WONKY WONDERLAND

MUSEUM OF MAGICAL ARTEFACTS
BOOK THREE

A.A. ALBRIGHT

This is a work of fiction. Names, characters, organisations, places, events and incidents are either products of the author's imagination, or are used fictitiously.

Text Copyright © A.A. Albright 2024
All Rights Reserved

No part of this book may be reproduced, or stored in a retrieval system, or transmitted by any form or by any means, electronic, mechanical, photocopying, recording, or otherwise, without express written permission of the author.

Website: https://aaalbright.com
Newsletter

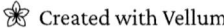 Created with Vellum

CHAPTER 1
THE DEEP END

If you've been with me for my previous adventures, then you'll already know this, but if not, then I'll just come out and say it – I'm a nerd. I have been a nerd my whole life long, and I will be one for the rest of my days. I *love* Magical History, and in an ideal world, my job at the Museum of Magical Artefacts would be my dream job.

But this world is very far from ideal.

And so, when I came into work this morning, just one day after the museum boss had sent me on a job that had almost killed me, I wasn't feeling like the happiest bunny in the warren.

I arrived two hours before opening time, hoping to avoid Hugo, Jake and Fee, and rushed straight for the museum's central tower, where I finally stopped rushing and sighed at the enormous statue of the Griffin.

The statue sighed back.

'What are *you* sighing for?' I asked him (because yes, he could talk – to me, at least).

'It seemed like the fashionable thing to do. Laine is in Ralph's office.'

'Yeah, I thought he might be,' I said. 'Are you going to slide over and let me up, or do we have to pretend I need to give you the password?'

He shook his regal-eagle head. 'I've never liked playing pretend, Annie. Save passwords for when others are about.'

Laine, the museum's treasure-hunting extraordinaire, was sitting behind Ralph's desk, reading something from a file. When I walked in, he closed the file and set it aside.

'I was wondering if you'd show up today,' he said, his voice sounding tired. He *looked* tired, too. There were dark circles below his hazel eyes, and his thick dark hair was in serious need of a comb. Normally, despite his adventure-guy style clothing, he seemed healthy and well-rested.

'No you weren't.'

'No,' he admitted. 'I wasn't. I guess I knew you'd show. You're going to do the job with me?'

Ah, the job. The reason I'd tossed and turned all night long. The reason I wanted to kick Ralph Murray, the museum boss, in his unmentionables. Because after I'd only narrowly escaped death, Ralph now wanted me to go on another no-doubt deadly errand. This time, though, he wasn't sending me there alone. This time, I would be working with Laine.

While treasure-hunting might be in Laine's job

description, it was definitely not in mine. I was a conservator of magical artefacts, and that was all I wanted to be. I'd had quite enough of tracking down powerful objects when I'd been at Crooked College, and I didn't want to do it again. People thought treasure hunting was exciting, and maybe it *was* if you were looking for pretty, non-magical treasures. But the objects which called out to me came along with a large heaping of danger.

Oh, I'd thought of the many ways in which I might say 'No,' to this latest job, and none of them were polite. I had every intention of saying all of those impolite things, too, just as soon as I could get out of Ralph's clutches. But now was not that time. I'd been told that this expedition would help me save Dora, my mysterious vanishing familiar. Ralph hadn't mentioned what it was that she needed saving *from,* but (as he no doubt intended, the sly old sod) I was far too curious to refuse the job.

'I mean, I think I made it clear that I was going to work with you on this,' I told Laine. 'Like I said last night, I don't really have a choice, do I?'

'Because of this Dora Ralph mentioned to me, right? Who is she, Annie? All Ralph told me was that this job would give you answers about her, and that it was the only way you could save her. It'll help me – it'll help *us* – if I know more.'

I gritted my teeth. It wasn't Laine's fault I distrusted him. He'd come through for me, after all, staging a rescue attempt when I was trapped in a flat with a murderous mummy, a curse-crazed weredog, and a bunch of creepy phantasms. And we had so much in common. Laine had similar powers to mine, and he was at Ralph's mercy too, reluctantly working for the museum so that its magic would keep his gifts a secret. Still, he'd known Ralph far longer than he'd known me. Until I could be sure where his loyalties lay, I was going to hold off on fully trusting him.

'It doesn't matter who Dora is,' I said.

'I think it does. But okay, you don't have to tell me yet. Honestly, I'm surprised you've come in this morning. I knew you'd do the job, but I thought you might need a little time to ... mentally adjust to the situation. I sure did. A few years ago, when it became very clear to me that working at the museum was the only way to keep my gifts a secret, I threw an almighty temper tantrum, which involved *not* coming into work and drinking a lot. I think I always knew I'd relent in the end and do whatever Ralph said, but ... being stuck here, subject to his every whim, it wasn't an easy situation for me to accept. You're far more sensible than me.'

'Yeah, I'm super sensible,' I drawled. 'So, come on, then. Out with it. What *is* this job? You might as well tell me, so we can get on with training.'

'And get it all over with as soon as possible?'

'I'm here, Laine. Isn't that enough? I'm not going to lie and tell you I'm looking forward to it.'

'Fair enough. My ego's survived worse, I suppose. Have you heard of Wonderland?'

'As in *Alice's Adventures in Wonderland*?'

'As in that, yeah. Well, Wonderland is very, very real. But that's not where we're going.'

'You are being very frustrating right now. But I think you know that.'

'Okay, okay, I'll just come out with it. We're going to a ... let's say a *warped* version of Wonderland, created by a vampire queen who was obsessed with Lewis Carroll's books. She calls her world Wonkyland, or sometimes Wonky Wonderland, or even Dark Wonderland, or ... well, look, by the time she was imprisoned there, she hadn't quite settled on a name.'

'Imprisoned?' I blinked at him.

'It all started off so innocently, you know – she was just your average evil vampire, luring seven-year-old girls into her world via portal mirrors and rabbit holes so she could play with them and drink their blood – or, if she really, really liked them, turn them into vampires so she could enjoy their company forever – but somewhere along the way, that sweet, harmless queen went sort of crazy.' He snorted, adding, 'Yeah, I'm being sarcastic.'

'Gee, really?'

'And it turns out sarcasm suits me better than it does you. But getting back to the subject at hand – Ciara, the vamp in question, was always evil. It took a while to deal with her. Firstly because time passes differently in her realm, so people were gone for days before anyone even knew they were missing. And secondly because she was so skilled at mind control that a lot of people were convinced that what she was doing was okay. But she was stopped in the end, and all of the rabbit holes and mirrors have been sealed up, sealing Ciara – AKA the Queen of Minds – inside.'

'How come I've never heard of this? I mean, seven-year-olds being kidnapped? Surely it would have made the news.'

'It probably did at the time. But it happened a hundred and twenty years ago, and there were all sorts of memory mods to wipe it from public knowledge. Officially, the only people who can get in or out of her realm now are a set of specially trained guards – their job is to make sure she's behaving, and not looking for a way out.'

'You said "officially" – has anyone else gone into the world?'

'I got the impression from Ralph's notes that someone might have gotten in there, about twenty years ago or thereabouts,' he replied. 'Though I can't say for sure, given that it's Ralph and he's not exactly forthcoming.'

'But how did they get in, if all of the ways in have been sealed? How are *we* supposed to get in – and why?'

'I think you can guess why.'

I didn't have to think about it for long. 'Ralph wants something that's in there, right?'

He gave me a curt nod. 'Got it in one – and you may as well file that answer away for future use, because you'll soon come to realise that Ralph *always* wants something. Here.' He fished about in his satchel and slid two books over to me. One was *Alice's Adventures in Wonderland,* the other *Through the Looking Glass.*

'I read them already,' I said. 'Granny was a bit of a rebel, you know, letting me read human books. Dad thoroughly disapproved.'

'Well, read them again. And again and again and again. We'll need to know these books back to front if we're to get in and out of Ciara's world in one piece.'

As I put the books in my bag, he stood up and walked

over to one of the many antique mirrors in the room. This one was a little taller than me, and was propped up against the wall. It was clean, but only because *I'd* been cleaning it – along with almost everything else in Ralph's office – for a while now.

'And according to Ralph,' he said, 'this is how we get in.'

I eyed the mirror with more than a touch of scepticism. 'So, you know I've been helping Hugo up here from time to time,' I began. 'Well, Ralph wants me to make it a more permanent arrangement, in fact, using some special solutions to make sure that the objects in here stay neutralised. The thing is, I haven't felt anything at all from this particular mirror. Even with the neutralising sprays I should feel *something,* shouldn't I?' I touched it now, focusing hard. 'But I can't. Can you?'

Laine put his hand next to mine and closed his eyes. 'No, I can't, actually. But Ralph assures me that this mirror is a portal to Wonky Wonderland. He says there's a key needed to activate it, and he'll give it to us when we're ready to go through. I imagine once it's activated, we'll both feel something. The problem is, what happens when we get there. Ralph says that this thing he wants, the Queen of Minds is protecting it, and she'll do her best to stop us getting it. Everyone and everything in that world will be working for her, doing her bidding.'

'There are others trapped in there?'

He nodded. 'Everyone innocent was evacuated before the prison world was sealed, so everyone who's there now is someone who worked for the Queen of Minds – supernaturals who were loyal to her and who helped her in her crimes. If they are all vamps, like they reportedly are, then your defensive skills will need to be spot on before we even attempt to enter. But maybe we have an ally in there. Dora.'

I shivered at the implication. If he was suggesting Dora was in there, then that would mean she had willingly worked for some crazed vampire queen. But she couldn't have, could she? She was too cute to be evil. 'How will we know when I'm ready?' I asked, avoiding the question. 'How will *he*?'

Laine lifted a brow. 'Like all my jobs for Ralph, I guess we'll be ready whenever he gets impatient. In the meantime...' He moved away from the mirror. 'Seeing as you're so enthusiastic, I guess we should get started with our training.'

He went back to the desk, reaching behind it and pulling a large leather suitcase onto the desk's surface. I sat across from him, waiting for him to open it – and waiting, and waiting...

While I waited, I spied two other new items on Ralph's desk. The first was a bronze bell, the kind you'd see at reception in an old-fashioned hotel. The second thing was a new snow globe. The globe was clumped in with what remained of his collection (a couple had been destroyed by a crazy murderous vampire – I was beginning to sense a theme), but it was definitely new. The snow scene inside was so beautiful, with a gorgeous little cottage looking cosy and warm, like a refuge from the snowstorm outside. I would have noticed something so lovely before.

Pointing to it, I asked, 'Is that what Ralph brought back from his most recent travels? Or the bell? Or both?'

Laine frowned. 'I guess both, maybe, but I don't really know. He comes back with mysterious boxes all the time but never tells me what's in them. What I do know is that the man is obsessed with snow globes, for some reason. Nothing in his collection is powerful, as far as I can tell. Just antiques – at best. I suspect quite a few of them are just cheap knick-knacks that took his fancy. Anyway, can we please focus on what I'm about to show you?'

'I'm focused, I'm focused. Jeez. Just open it already.'

He moved his hand to the lock on the case, and I heard a click. Pulling up the lid, he turned it to face me. The suitcase was lined with wands. Old, rough-looking wands, each one gnarlier than the next. Despite the dust and the dirt on them, despite the fact that some were splintered, I could tell that they were powerful – very, very powerful.

'I can see that you don't use a lot of magic, Annie. It's inside you, obviously – you broke the curse on that locket around your neck, so I *know* you're powerful.' His eyes settled, for a moment, on the Locket of Longing.

I covered it with my hand, disliking the way he was staring. Ralph had wanted to buy it from the revived mummy who owned it, but she had refused to sell it to him, and given it to me instead. Laine told me the only reason Ralph wanted to buy it was so *he* could gift it to me. I wasn't sure whether to believe him, but if Ralph *did* want to act like Mister Magnanimous, then he probably had a darker motive.

'But there's something about the kind of power you and I have,' Laine continued, tearing his eyes from the jewellery. 'It's like ... we want to hide it so bad we wind up hiding all of our other magics, too. Where we're going, we can't afford for you to be afraid, Annie. You need to be able to unlock that magic. But that'll take a lot of work, and for this first job of ours, we simply don't have enough time. So I'm going to teach you to channel. Each of these wands has a vast power of its own. Power that *you* can channel, and direct where you need.'

'You're teaching me wizardry?'

'I'm going to teach you a lot, Annie. But yeah, wizardry is where we start. Touch every wand in this case, and pick the most powerful.'

I ran my hand along the line of wands, already knowing the most powerful among them – a short, wonky, splintered looking one at the far end of the case, second up from the bottom. It was crying out to my mind, telling me that we could do wonderful things together. Of course, it wanted me to *begin* our wonderful journey by sending a death spell Laine's way.

As I passed over it and focused on the other wands, I soon realised almost *all* had ill intent. And many of them ... many of them were a horrible shade of green, a shade which made me recall the phantasms my locket produced when it was cursed.

Finally, I found one that shone with a different colour – a white light, but a white which shimmered, as though made up of every single colour possible. It felt peaceful, promising rather than ominous, so I picked it up. It felt good in my hands. It felt almost ... familiar. It was a fairly straight wand, made of hawthorn.

Laine's brow furrowed. 'Why that one?'

'Because it's the only one that doesn't want me to kill you,' I replied, speaking the truth but not the whole truth. 'But if you do have a death wish, I can happily pick up another.'

'Seriously? But I've trained with all of these wands myself.'

'Yeah? Maybe that's why they don't like you.'

He shrugged. 'You think you can work with that one, fine. Funnily enough, that's the one Ralph thought you'd pick.'

'Oh.' I looked down at my chosen wand with suspicion. Now that I knew Ralph wanted me to pick it, I wished I'd picked something else.

'Now, next of all ...' Laine steepled his fingers, surveying me seriously. 'This central tower, it's ... not all that it seems. There are rooms below this one, but you need to have the key before they'll reveal themselves.' He pulled out the layer of wands, and below it was a layer of golden keys, nine in total, each one with a label tied to its neck. Laine took out the key labelled *Room No. 1*.

'Don't even bother trying to touch the others,' he said. 'If you've not been authorised to touch them, they'll burn a pattern into your palm. And only Ralph has the balm that can erase it.'

'Spoken like a man with experience.'

He looked down at his palm. 'It was a painful lesson, yeah. Come on. I'll show you.'

He stood up and rushed from the room, bounding

down the steps and heading out to Hugo's office area. The Griffin closed behind us.

'Okay, I know that this Griffin looks like nothing but a statue,' he said. 'But there's definitely some sentience here. It can understand the password, obviously, but ... I dunno. I think it's more than that. You ever feel something from it?'

'Um ... maybe,' I hedged. My relationship with the Griffin didn't feel like something I wanted to share right now – and definitely not with Laine. 'I haven't really thought about it.'

'You haven't? That surprises me. I've thought about this Griffin a *lot* since the moment I first saw it. It's like ... I keep waiting for it to say something more to me. I mean, it burned that guy Thorn's beard, didn't it, when he tried to sneak up to the tower? Anyway, I want to see if this works for you, so hold the key up in front of the statue while you say the latest password. I gave it to you along with Ralph's schedule, didn't I?'

'Yeah, you did.' I held the key aloft and said, 'Michaelmas.'

The Griffin slid aside, saying nothing. But now that the tower was open once more, I could see the same staircase I'd seen during my first time here – the stairs leading *down*.

'Each key unlocks a different level,' Laine explained, bounding down the steps to the landing below, stopping in front of a thick metal door. There was gold lettering upon it, which, like the label on the key, read: *Room No.1*. 'Believe it or not, the stairs go *much* further down than this.'

'Wow, really?' I tried to keep my expression neutral. Laine didn't appear to be hearing what I was hearing – something much further below us was calling my name. I was experiencing a mind-assault of images, too: images of a battle, of flames, and now – something which hadn't been there before – an image of *me,* travelling quickly through the sky and looking at the ground far below. And there was a sound as I travelled, a sound like beating wings.

'So, now you just have to stick the key in the door.'

Shaking the visions from my mind, I did as he suggested, putting the key in the lock and turning it. With a click, the heavy metal door swung open. Inside I saw a large, dark room with stone floors. Sconces on the wall suddenly flared to life, giving enough light for me to see the mats arranged on the floor – they looked like gym mats, maybe – and, worse than that, the weapons on the far wall. There were swords, daggers, spears, throwing stars and darts. There were nunchaku and maces, an enormous selection of ropes and chains, and even a section of what seemed to be antique guns.

'We'll get to the weapons later in the week,' Laine said, following my gaze. 'For the first couple of days we're going to stick to a combination of fitness – so you can run like the wind if needs be – and simple Defensive Magic like teleportation and blocking spells.'

'Simple,' I muttered, my voice sounding thin and scared. 'Sure. I'm great at those *simple* spells.'

'Well, I know you're not, but you could be, if you just opened up to your magic a bit more. But like I said, we don't have time for that just now. You'll have no trouble with them as long as you keep that wand in your hand. So. Ready?'

Before I could tell him that I definitely wasn't ready, he was talking again. 'The basic command for *block* is actually like telling something or someone to get away in Irish,' he informed me.

'*Imigh?*'

'Exactly. That wand should make it simple enough, if it's as powerful as Ralph seems to think it is. After a while, you should form a bond – you'll get to a point where all you have to do is *think* a command, and the wand carries it out. Okay?'

'Okay.' I nodded nervously. I didn't want to form a bond with a sentient wand, because films and books had taught me that such things could get very creepy. What I wanted was to grow a bond with Dora, my familiar. But if going into this prison world was the only way I could see the mysterious dormouse again – and help her, if she needed it – then I knew I'd better be prepared. And if Dora, the cutest creature in the world, turned out to be just as evil as the vampire queen, well ... I'd better be prepared for that, too.

'*Conáil*,' Laine shouted.

I raised my wand and shouted '*Imigh*,' but I was a moment too late, and he managed to freeze me. I couldn't move. I struggled to even think, until he mobilised me once more.

'It is not nice being frozen,' I remarked. 'But it's not cold, at least.'

He chuckled. 'No. It's not that kind of freezing. Wayfarers, and most people using defensive spells, they just want to incapacitate a person long enough to stop them doing harm. They don't want to give them hypothermia. Though I believe there are some spells that can *actually* freeze a person, I don't think any of Queen Ciara's minions will send those your way.'

'You don't? Why not?'

He shrugged. 'Ralph seems to think they'll want to capture us, not injure us. He does suggest we get this right, though, before we move onto hand-to-hand combat. Not all of her minions will use magic. Some of them will use force.'

I warily eyed the weapons. 'Are all expeditions like this? I mean, do you have to defend yourself a lot? Because–'

'Because you thought the stories I told were crap, right?'

'Well, I mean ... kraken.'

'Are very, very real, and I have endured some pretty scary fights with them, more than once. And yes, a lot of jobs are dangerous. This one ... something about the instructions Ralph gave – I'm afraid it might be more dangerous than anything I've done so far.'

'So, a perfect job for a novice like me.'

He shot me a wry grin. 'Nothing like jumping in at the deep end.'

CHAPTER 2
DREAMS OF WONDERLAND

We went on that way for over a week, until I was so wrecked that my muscles forgot to ache. Lessons with Laine, work in the museum, reading *Alice's Adventures in Wonderland* and *Through the Looking Glass* over and over and over again ... it all blurred together into one excruciating and exhausting mess, until I wasn't even sure what day it was.

If Queen Ciara's wonky version of Wonderland was anything like the worlds in Lewis Carroll's stories, I couldn't see any way of getting through this task successfully. The books were like dreams, with Alice gliding from one strange set of creatures to another, on and on until she woke up.

But Laine and I wouldn't be able to wake up. We'd have to make sense of the strangeness all around us if we were ever going to bring back what Ralph wanted – and I still didn't know what that might be.

You would think, given how tired I was, that sleeping

would have been my favourite thing. But it wasn't – because whenever I *did* snatch a few hours of sleep, Lewis Carroll's stories invaded my dreams.

It wasn't only Lewis Carroll's worlds I was dreaming about, though – soon, I began to dream about the world I was preparing to enter with Laine. In those dreams I was face to face with the vampire queen. She had long, crimson red hair. She wore a ruby crown and a smirk, while Dora snoozed in a teapot beside her.

The teapot was white, with playing card symbols painted upon it. The strangest thing about the dream, though, was that in it, Hugo was standing by my side. He looked younger – we both did. He was maybe eleven or twelve, while I looked around seven. We were holding hands and shivering as we stood in front of the Queen. Whenever I woke from those dreams, I continued to shiver for a good long while.

To my own surprise I was getting better at defensive spells – the wand helped a lot, and so did Laine's training. Part of me was happy about that, part of me was terrified; I feared that if I did well on this job, Ralph would send me on another, and then another. He seemed like the kind of guy who would always want something else.

But once I had Dora back – you know, if she *wasn't* an evil chum of Queen Ciara's – then I would come up with a plan to deal with Ralph. I wanted to stay at the museum, I really did – I just didn't want threats hanging over my head, and I certainly didn't want to go on any more dangerous jobs. What I needed was to get some dirt on him. Something I could use against him, something to out-threaten his threat to expose me. But as to how I would get that dirt ... well, I was at a loss.

I barely saw my mother – sometimes a quick greeting in the morning or a 'G'night,' on the way past if she happened to be awake when I got home and fell into bed. Finally, a morning off arrived, but I wouldn't get to catch up on my sleep. Instead, I was about to do something I hadn't told anybody about: I was going to pay a visit to the fae realm, to see their queen. In a vision I'd experienced, I'd learned that she forged the Locket of Longing. If anyone could explain its mysteries, it would be her.

Ever since the ghost-man had saved my skin, the locket had been quiet. The ghost hadn't appeared again, and I was afraid to try to force him. From what I understood, my locket was a conduit between this life and the next; it wasn't something I was willing to mess about with just to satisfy my own curiosity. But I really wished I were a less sensible person, because my need to know more about my ghost-man was *bad*.

When I got up that morning I moved around the flat as quietly as I could, getting my stuff together for the trip I was about to take. Finally, after years of being useless at Travelling spells, I'd mastered them in my lessons with Laine. Admittedly it was all down to the new wand, rather than my own burgeoning skills. But while I had it, I intended to take advantage.

I was just about to use it to head to my destination, when I heard my mother screaming, 'Annie! Annie, I need you!'

I checked my watch. I wanted to get to the fae realm early, but I couldn't ignore my mother – not unless I wanted to endure about a month of passive-aggressiveness in return.

When I walked into the Hungry Hippy's kitchen, I saw that we had a visitor: Chickpea, my father's familiar. The beige-coloured cat was halfway through a plate of roast beef.

'Is Dad here?' I asked, unable to hide my involuntary judder.

Chickpea glanced my way. 'Windflower is busy with important work this morning, so I've come to help Iris out with this leftover beef. I wouldn't eat meat otherwise, you know – I'm a vegetarian.'

'Uh-huh.' I couldn't deal with my father's crazy cat right now – I was just grateful that Dad wasn't with him. Although, now that I thought about it, Dad hadn't been around here for a few days. At first, when Mam won the latest coven election and knocked Dad off the top spot, he had come round to complain a lot – usually he'd turn up late in the evening, swigging wine from a bottle and telling my mother that she'd regret usurping him. He'd even threatened to sue her (what legal grounds he had were anyone's guess). But for the past few days, he'd been conspicuous by his absence.

'Everything okay?' I questioned my mother.

'Not really.' She lifted up Chickpea, along with his plate of roast beef, and deposited both outside the back door. Only when she'd shut the cat outside did she point at the oven and say, 'It's not working.'

I narrowed my eyes. 'You didn't try baking bran muffins again, did you?'

'No! I've learned my lesson where bran muffins are

concerned. I put blueberry muffins in, along with a breakfast tray bake – you know the one the customers love, where it's like a big thick omelette with lots of peppers, and chunks of chorizo.'

'Hm. The oven normally loves making that.' I approached it, touching it cautiously. It hadn't even warmed up yet, though my mother had definitely switched the dial to *On*.

'Huh, that's strange,' I mused. 'It's showing me pictures of Fee, baking a lentil loaf.' Like my father's cat, Fee remained convinced that she could eat nothing but vegetarian food. Werewolves and vegetarianism did not go paw in paw, but Fee was giving it a good go. 'Was she working here last night?'

'She had a shift, yeah. But lentil loaf wasn't on the menu.'

'Hm. Y'know, I don't think the lentil loaf Fee was baking is Granny's recipe. What the oven is showing me is a kind of a beige mush of a thing. It looks more like one of Dad's recipes than Gran's. Plus, the oven is giving me the sense that Fee was cooking it for herself.'

'Why would the oven be showing you that? Is it telling tales on her?' She crossed her arms and looked angrily at the oven. 'Look here, you, I don't care if Fee cooks things for herself. I've told her she's very welcome to make whatever she wants in this kitchen.'

'It's not telling tales,' I said, giving the oven a reassuring smile. 'Or not in the way you think, anyway. I'm getting the sense that it's looking *out* for Fee. Like it's worried about her, and it wants me to know. Our oven likes Fee a lot, from what it's showing me. I feel a lot of emotion towards her.' I touched it softly. 'You're ever so sweet, aren't you?'

I felt it begin to warm up beneath my touch. 'It should be fine, now it's told me what it wanted to. Just keep an eye on Fee, maybe, whenever she's due in here next. The oven really is concerned about her.'

My mother checked that all was well with her muffins and tray bake before saying, 'You know, I can understand why the oven's worried, now that I think about it. I mean, Fee's the best employee I've ever had – I wish she was fulltime here instead of only weekends and evenings. But maybe she's doing too much, Annie. She has been looking tired this week. Last night there were actually a couple of occasions when I thought she might faint. I told her to go home, but she refused. Look, you'll be seeing her before I will, won't you? When you get into work, ask her if everything's okay. And tell her I'll understand if she needs to take time off.'

'Yeah, I'll see what I can do. Got to go.'

'You're leaving awfully early again. Another Pilates class?'

That had been my excuse for my recent early mornings, so I said, 'Yeah – a strong core is super-important, you know.'

Her frown was a deep one, making great furrows on her usually smooth forehead. 'Annie, your Pilates teacher came in for lunch yesterday, and told me you've missed your last two classes. If you're going out for breakfast with this treasure hunter fella, why don't you just say so? There's nothing wrong with having a boyfriend. Although I did think you had a bit of a thing for Jake.'

I swallowed and looked away. 'Fine, I'm having breakfast with Laine. But honestly, it's just so we can chat about work stuff. He and I are working on a big project together for the museum.'

'Hm.' She seemed unconvinced. 'Well, bring him over for dinner sometime so I can decide what I think of him. So far, all I'm thinking is that he's monopolising far too much of your time.'

As I turned to leave, she grabbed me, turning me around and pulling the wand from my back pocket. 'Where'd you get this?'

'It's a loaner, from work. You know I'm not very good at things like levitation spells, and I need to use them for moving big objects. The wand helps.'

'It looks ...' Her forehead furrowed again. 'It looks familiar. It's just like one you had when you were little.'

'What?' I took it from her hands and looked it over. 'I never had one like this. I remember having a bright orange training wand when I was at school.'

'Oh, you had one of those, but only *after* you lost this one. Your granny gave you this one as a gift, and you absolutely loved it. Then one day you came back from an outing with Windflower crying that you'd lost it. It was the strangest thing. You couldn't remember what happened, but Windflower said he'd taken you to the museum, and you must have lost it there. He and I had a huge fight about it. You'd already started to display unusual magic where objects were concerned, so it was the last place I wanted him taking you. But you ... it was so strange, Annie. It wasn't just that you forgot how you lost your wand. You seemed to forget that you were even in the museum.'

I didn't like *any* of what she'd just said, not one little bit. I wasn't the sort of person to forget much, even from an early age. I fully remembered other awful days out with Windflower, right down to the terrible food he'd tried to make me eat on each occasion. So why not this trip to the museum? And if this was my wand, shouldn't *I* have recognised it?

'Well ... it can't be my lost wand,' I said. 'That would just be too big of a coincidence.'

'Not *that* big, when you think about it. Maybe it went into some lost and found box, and it's been there all this time.'

That suitcase had not been a lost and found box. Not unless almost every wand lost in the museum happened to have dark intent and an eagerness to murder Laine. He was annoying, sure – but not *that* annoying. 'Yeah, yeah that must be it,' I said uneasily. 'Huh. Weird.'

'Weird is right. I don't like the sound of this, Annie – it's making me feel itchy and uncomfortable, and I don't quite know *why*, which makes me feel even *more* itchy and uncomfortable. Look, Ralph hasn't been asking you to do any unusual jobs, has he? He hasn't shown any sign that he knows what you can do?'

'No,' I lied. 'He hasn't. Look, I'd better go, or I'll be late.'

THESE DAYS, THERE WERE A FEW ENTRANCES YOU COULD TAKE to the fae realm, but I'd chosen one right on the other side of Ireland. Not because I'm a martyr (though I sometimes wondered), but because it was the entrance where I was least likely to bump into anyone I knew. My dad still had a small handful of loyal Egans, and they were awfully keen on the wholefood shops in the faery realm.

I *thought* my destination would be easy enough. The wand took me directly to a forest called the Wandering Wood, where the door to the realm was said to be situated at a hawthorn tree. But for those of you who've never visited the Wandering Wood, my advice is: don't. Magical forests that move around willy-nilly aren't half as fun as they sound.

There were plenty of signposts saying *Door to Fae Realm This Way.* The problem was, each sign pointed in a totally different direction. It couldn't actually be down every single path, could it?

Time was ticking on, so I chose a direction at random – and my choice was not a good one. I passed the same duck pond five times, and took a bridge over the same river at least twice, but eventually I came to a point where the forest grew thinner, and a cliff sloped down to the sea. There I saw it: a huge hawthorn tree, with a queue of waiting people.

I joined the queue, craning my neck until I saw the doorway that would lead me into the fae realm – it was a shimmering silver arch that looked like it was made from the roots of the tree itself. It shone so brightly that I couldn't make out what might lie on the other side.

When my turn came, a tall, ethereally good-looking

woman looked me up and down. 'Purpose of your visit to the fae realm?'

'Educational,' I said, just as I'd rehearsed in my head a hundred times last night, and another thousand times during my slog through the woods. 'Visiting the Museum of Never Again.'

'Come through, then.' With the barest touch of her fingers, she opened the shining doorway, revealing a matching forest beyond. 'You'll need a taxi to get to the museum.' She beckoned a dark-haired man who was leaning against a nearby tree. 'Brecon! Brecon, we've got a girl needing a taxi.'

As Brecon strode over to me, I soon realised that he wasn't fae, but Púca – because when he was about three feet away from me, he seamlessly transformed into a sleek black horse and said, 'Hop on, beautiful.'

With a shudder, I awkwardly scrambled onto his back. It wasn't that I was unused to Púca men – we had Rowan at the museum, running an exhibition – but I'd never seen Rowan shift, and he certainly hadn't asked me if I'd like a ride. Still, when in Faeryland...

CHAPTER 3
THE MUSEUM OF NEVER AGAIN

Riding a Púca, it turned out, was not a fun experience. I was a girl who'd vomited when my flying teacher forced me to take my broom more than a foot off the ground. And if I thought a broom was bad, a Púca ride was much, much worse. There was a blinding flash of light, and then the world went upside down and inside out. My stomach churned, and I saw all sorts of colours blurring in front of my eyes. It reminded me of the time I'd accidentally eaten one of Windflower's 'special' jellies.

I didn't throw up, but it took an iron will not to. With another flash of light, Brecon finally came to a stop in front of a towering building made of wood and stone. He was apparently used to turning people's stomachs, because he gave me plenty of time to clumsily dismount; he politely chewed some grass for a minute or two while I got myself together.

'How much do I owe you?' I asked, once he'd shifted

from impossibly attractive horse into impossibly attractive man.

'You don't.' He winked at me. 'Your rides today have been paid for by Her Majesty. I'll come back to fetch you once you're done – she says she'll meet you inside.'

He transformed again and galloped off, leaving me standing there like some sort of witch-guppy hybrid, mouth wide open, memory shot. Sure, it had been a strange journey, but we hadn't *talked* along the way, had we? How did he know I was hoping to meet the faery queen? How did *she* know?

As I entered the museum on shaky legs, I stared all around me at the vast space. I *knew* I was inside – I could see the beams of the ceiling far above me – but I had never before been in an inside that felt so much like an outside. The wood in this place was (literally) alive, covered with moss, leaves and branches. There were even sweet-smelling flowers and yummy-looking fruits hanging down.

Countless hordes of sprites zipped in and out of the greenery. I could see tiny treehouses with doors and verandas. On one veranda, an old sprite was sitting on a rocking chair, smoking a pipe. On another, a buff young sprite was lifting weights.

I was so stunned by the sprites that it took me a moment to notice not everything around me was lovely. Slowly, the exhibits on the walls seeped into my consciousness, making me feel a little sick. There were pictures of bloody battle scenes from wars that had rocked the magical world, alongside the dark objects used at the time. Below each painting or object, there were horrifically detailed descriptions of the events.

A great painting called *The Battle of the Wandering Wood* was hung in a place of pride. The battle had happened quite recently, in the area around the hawthorn tree I'd come through today. Vampires and witches had joined forces in order to destroy the fae. In the painting, a small group was at the centre of an enormous battle – a man and woman, dressed like the campest vampires ever, seemed to be facing off against a heroic threesome, made up of a gorgeous bleach-haired guy, a beautiful redhead and a stubborn-looking blonde lady.

'The stubborn-looking woman is my granddaughter,' said a voice behind me. 'I'm ever so proud of her. She reminds me of how I was, at her age.'

I jumped, finding myself face to face with the woman I'd seen in my recent vision: the Queen of the Sióga. I knew she must be thousands of years old, at least, but she didn't look much older than me. She was beautiful, with long titian hair and kind eyes. She wore a long white dress, and her feet were bare. She looked like she should be off frolicking in a field of flowers somewhere, rather than ruling the most powerful realm in the world.

Extending a hand, she said, 'Annie Divine, I presume. I've been waiting to meet you.'

'Egan,' I corrected nervously. Divine was my grandfather's name. It was weird enough that the Griffin sometimes called me that, but this woman too?

'Ah. My mistake. Come. I have a meeting with one of my guards in ten minutes. We can talk until he gets here.'

She led me to a cushioned circular sofa. From where we sat, I could see through an archway into a smaller hall. A sign above the arch told me that it was the Prison Worlds Exhibition.

My stomach lurched. Laine and I were planning on going to a prison world, and now I was only a few feet away from an exhibition on that very subject. I wanted, so much, to ask her what she knew about Queen Ciara's world. But Ralph wouldn't be happy if I blabbed about my upcoming expedition. Still, I couldn't stop myself from peeking through that arch.

On the far wall, behind thickened glass, there was a tea set. Maybe it wasn't a *set,* exactly – it was mismatched, to say the very least. But there was everything one might need for a March Hare's get-together: silver spoons, knives to cut the bread and cake and spread the butter, a sugar bowl, a milk jug, a teapot and some cups, saucers and plates. At the sight of the teapot and cups, I felt another nervous lurch in my belly. The cups were blue with red hearts, just like Dora's, and the pot was white, with playing card symbols upon it, like the one I'd been dreaming of this week.

'You look as if you've seen a ghost,' said the Queen. 'It can be that way, in this little museum of mine. I call it the Museum of Never Again because it was my great hope that these reminders of wars past would prevent the same from happening in the future. I think ... I think I got it wrong, Miss Egan. I think what the world needs now is a Museum of Hopes and Possibilities.'

I blinked at her. I'd never met a woman quite like her before. I couldn't decide if I found her lovely or discomfiting. There was no doubt that she *looked* lovely, bare feet aside. But she was supposed to be the most powerful supernatural around. If she made mistakes, what hope was there for the rest of us?

'Or perhaps the ghost you're seeing is not the ghost of war, but the ghost who visits you through this locket,' she went on, reaching out to touch the jewellery around my neck. 'You know, I suppose, that I forged this.'

'I do,' I admitted. 'It's why I'm here. But I guess you already knew that, seeing as you seem to know everything.'

'I dreamt you'd come here, and now you have. In my dream, you asked me who your ghost-man was. You told me he'd saved your skin, but you had no knowledge of who he might be. You don't feel any connection to him?'

'I mean ... I like him. He makes me feel safe or something. Or ... he did. I can't really feel him for the last few days, to be honest. But when I could, I felt like he was good, and like ... like I *should* have known him, but I didn't. I've never even seen a photo of this man, Your Majesty, let alone met him. And he's not the kind of guy you'd forget if you did meet him, y'know? He has this crazy wild hair – grey, but maybe it was sort of reddish or strawberry blond when he was younger. Wild blue eyes. He looks kind of crazed, in a way, but ... not scary. This locket is meant to connect you to someone you've loved and lost, right? So shouldn't I at least *know* him?'

'That is the purpose of the locket, yes. It's a bridge between this life and what comes next, and it is a bridge which only forms when someone loves the other dearly.

Although ...' Her face grew sheepish. '... I *have* heard tell that some horrible Pookeen queen subverted it into something ugly for a while. Well done on breaking her curse, by the way.'

'Oh, that was down to the Wayfarers,' I told her, lying through my deceitful teeth.

'Really?' She looked about as dubious as she ought to. 'Well, that aside, can you think of no one at all that you might not recognise, but who could care about you all the same?'

My mind went to Sir Blake Bingley. My connection with him had felt ever so real. 'There's someone. Someone whose face I didn't see. But even though I kind of wish it might be him, I just don't know, Your Majesty. I mean, the guy I'm thinking about was around in medieval times. Whereas this guy, this ghost who helped me, he was wearing a suede jacket and jeans.' Also, I didn't add, I didn't feel remotely attracted to him. 'Can ghosts choose their outfit? Maybe they like to move with the times?'

She laughed lightly. 'Not usually, no. They most often appear in whatever they died in. Though some very powerful ghosts can appear however they wish, I'm doubtful that's what's happening here. You're thinking of the knight, yes? Sir Blake Bingley? The story of a suit of armour coming to life was gossiped about in *all* the realms. I imagine Ralph Murray is happy. Notoriety for the museum means footfall for the museum, yes?'

'Yeah, Ralph loves any kind of publicity, from what I can tell,' I agreed. 'This ghost, though, he could touch stuff. He had, like, a proper fight and everything. And he did a sealing spell on a door. I could ...' I hesitated about whether to tell her this next part. In the end, my hope that she might be able to explain it made me talk. 'I could see the magic he used. I'm not supposed to see magic.'

'Pass me your locket awhile, Annie. I'll try to connect with it, and we'll see what I can divine.'

I did as she requested. 'And the magic I saw?' I asked.

'There are two possibilities where that's concerned. The first is that the curse *changed* the locket so much that seeing the colour of magic became possible, as far as those magics which were a result of it. Tell me, how did the curse make the phantasms look – those fake ghosts it used to control people, I mean – were they very convincing?'

'Not to me. They were green.'

'And during your time at the museum, have you seen or sensed anything ... unusual? Do you ever, perhaps, see a glow around certain objects?'

I swallowed, looking away from her. 'I thought I saw a green glow around some wands. It was very faint, though.'

She nodded decisively. 'You *are* a Divine, just as I thought. Henry's granddaughter, if I am not mistaken. He was a lovely man.'

My eyes darted all around. Touching my arm softly, she said, 'I am Queen of the Sióga. There is nothing that the magic of your museum can keep from *me*. But I shall certainly keep your secret safe. Annie, some very rare witches – and others, too – have gifts which they should not have. Gifts which are similar to magic that the fae have. Sometimes it's because there is fae ancestry somewhere along the line, sometimes it's because a gift has been made by a faery to a witch. It's even rarer, but not unheard of, for those gifts to manifest again in further generations. Music is the magic we love the most, so if we happen upon a witch or a human who plays in a way we like, we sometimes give them some extra oomph in that area – you'll have come across people whose music is transcendent, no doubt. But *you* have a different sort of fae-given gift, I think. A gift which was given to the Divine coven long ago, and which you inherited from Henry, involving magical objects. Yes?'

'Yes,' I said, my voice shaking. It seemed silly to go on lying to a woman who knew everything.

'Well, knowing what I do of your museum, it will do a very good job of hiding any gifts you have where objects are concerned. That said, I'd advise you to keep anything regarding being fae-touched well and truly to yourself. People are wary of anything connected to my people and their power. So ... you may not know this, but as your grandfather's gift developed, as he honed it and used it daily, he began to see the colours of certain magics, almost as clearly as a fae might see them. Not always, and he wasn't always certain of what he was seeing. But, like the fae, he began to see dark magic in a particular shade of green.'

'Oh,' I whispered. 'And I saw ... a whitish magic on the locket, and on the spell this ghost-man did to seal the door when he was helping me.'

'Pure white?'

'No. Well, I thought it was at first, but then I saw that it shimmered with lots of different colours. Pearlescent, maybe you'd call it. But also, somehow, it was the purest white I'd ever seen. I saw it on this wand, too.' I pulled out the wand I'd been using.

'Interesting,' she said, taking the wand into her free hand and scrutinising it carefully. 'You're right about this magic, and I can assure you that this is a very good wand, and will do you no harm. It was fae made, in fact. This whitish magic you're seeing is how most would describe the magic which comes from my people.'

'But ... my mother is convinced this was a wand my granny gave me when I was a kid. Not that I can remember having it back then. I got it last week from some suitcase filled with wands in the museum.'

'Hm. Curiouser and curiouser. Perhaps you should ask your grandmother about it. Now, as to your ghost-man...'

She passed both wand and locket back to me. 'I'm afraid I cannot see him. But going on your description, I can tell you that he is not Sir Blake Bingley. When Blake died, he had sandy blond hair. And *such* a singing voice.'

'And blue eyes?'

'Yes.' She laughed. 'Exceptionally blue. How did you know that?'

'Well, he had kind of blue orbs when he was – when his suit of armour was brought to life. He was good-looking, wasn't he?'

'He was one of those men who's so good looking it's hard to look them in the eye. Almost as handsome as my husband Finvarra.'

'Yeah, I thought he might be,' I said with a half-hearted chuckle. 'Oh, Your Majesty, I just ... I'd hoped you could tell me more about the ghost.'

'I understand your thirst to know, believe me. Things in your life seem so out of control now, I sense. You think if you can understand at least this one thing, everything else will seem far less daunting. But you will know more, soon enough, I imagine. For now, all I can tell you is that he's not a typical ghost. He is not even typical for this locket. He should be able to communicate with *me,* for a start. Even though his connection is with you, this locket is my creation. It always gives me the answers I seek. He is trying, very hard, but something is preventing full communication. I feel, though, that he wants to protect you from something. Something he worries about, in the past and in the future.'

'In the past *and* in the future?'

'Not very helpful, I know, but it is the answer I'm receiving. And as for the strength he showed, well, that *is* typical for this locket. The ghosts who come through it, the bond they have with the locket's wearer, it makes for a stronger connection to the physical world than usual. It creates a bond such as a witch might have with their familiar – the sort of bond that transcends everything. Worlds, realms, nothing can get in the way of the witch-familiar bond, and – usually – nothing can get in the way of the bond created by this locket.'

A piece of paper and quill appeared in her hand, and she scribbled some words. When she was done, I thought she'd hand it to me, but instead she rolled it up, sang a pretty note, and the page disappeared.

'I have just sent a letter to a very talented woman,' she said. 'She has quite the way with ghosts. As soon as she can, I'm sure she'll be in touch with you. But ... *this* ghost ... I think even she will struggle. Still, there is one other thing I can tell you about him, and it is that he cares deeply for you. You may not know him, but he loves you all the same.'

I wasn't sure why, but her words made me feel a little weepy. They also made me more curious than ever. All in all, I felt just as mixed up as I had on arrival. There was no time for me to ask her anymore, though.

A man was approaching, and there was something so twitchy about his face. He had huge white sideburns which grew all the way into a whiskery moustache, and he walked across the floor with strange little hops. His uniform was strange, too; it was old-fashioned and almost whimsical, with a pale blue tailcoat and top hat, and a frilled white shirt. He even wore white leather gloves.

'Ah, Mr Coneen, here you are,' she said with a smile, standing up to greet him. To me, she added, 'Mr Coneen heads up the White Rabbit Guard. They're ... a special branch, you might say, overlooking things for me in another realm.'

My eyes rounded at that. A guard? There were plenty of guards lining the main hall, watching the visitors carefully. They were dressed in shining metallic-looking rigouts, while this guy looked like he was on his way to a tea party in the eighteen hundreds.

'The others are arriving presently, Your Majesty,' he said, nodding towards the arch into the Prison Worlds

Exhibition. I followed his gaze, and sure enough three more men appeared – they arrived suddenly, accompanied by a crack in the air, almost as if they'd popped into existence. They were dressed like Mr Coneen, and they looked just as twitchy.

'As I said to you in my recent letter,' he continued, 'we *need* to check the items. Immediately. Someone in one of the units is a rogue agent, Your Majesty, a rogue of the highest order, and–' He glanced at me and broke off. 'You're still here? Why are you still here?'

I blinked at him, unsure of how to answer that, and also a little dumbstruck by his eyes. They were pink.

'Don't be rude, Mr Coneen,' said the Queen. 'Annie is a welcome guest of mine. We were just finishing up.'

'Yeah, I'd better be leaving,' I said awkwardly, edging away. 'Thank you for ... well, for everything, Your Majesty.'

'You are very welcome, Annie. I hope you shall soon discover all of the answers you seek.'

I nodded and mumbled another thanks, as Mr Coneen began to march-hop through the archway, and the Queen followed him on her bare feet, smiling serenely.

I walked slowly out, my ears paying close attention to their conversation, as Mr Coneen exclaimed, 'You see, Your Majesty. It's all been stolen, the entire set, and replaced with fakes! And I know who did it, too. I–'

Mr Coneen stopped dead, and with a roil of dread in the pit of my belly, I ran back to see what was going on. He was on the ground in front of the tea set exhibit, clutching his chest.

The other twitchy guards all looked at one another, then one of them plucked a long, white hair from his moustache and hurled it at the ground. The hair was sharper than it looked, piercing the stone floor and creating a huge, swirling hole. The three of them jumped into it, and the hole vanished along with them.

CHAPTER 4
DENIAL, DENIAL...

I was steered out of the museum along with the other visitors, but not before I caught a good long look at Mr Coneen. His hand had flopped to the side, no longer clutching at his chest. His pink eyes were wide open, with no life in them. The Queen knelt over him, touching his chest and humming a tune. She didn't look confident. A tear slid down her cheek, turning solid midair and breaking like glass against Mr Coneen's body.

I wished I could stay and find out more, but the museum guards weren't the sort of people you'd want to argue with. Anyway, the same Púca-shifter-taxi guy who'd taken me here was waiting right outside.

'I think one of the White Rabbit Guard members was just killed,' I said, my voice coming out faint and shaky. 'Or at least hurt very badly.'

'Oh, dear.' Brecon's once cheeky expression was washed away by worry. 'Well, I'm sure our good queen will do whatever she can. Come. It's time for you to leave the realm.'

I was still eager to find my way back into the museum – maybe hang around until things calmed down and see if I could speak with the Queen again – but the Púca quickly transformed, then stamped his hooves impatiently.

'Hint taken,' I said with a sigh, as I ungracefully manoeuvred myself onto his back. My mind was so busy with it all that, this time around, I forgot to feel sick. I wished I knew what had happened in there, and what had been stolen from the Prison Worlds Exhibition.

Whatever it was, it was giving me a very strong dose of the heebie-jeebies. The coincidences were stacking far too high today. Something getting nicked from that particular exhibition, just as Laine and I were preparing for a trip *to* a prison world – how likely was that? And then there was the fact that the teacups behind the glass were just like Dora's, and the teapot was the same as the one in my dreams.

'See all you wanted to see?' Brecon asked me as he dropped me by the hawthorn tree and shifted back into his perfect manly form. The hawthorn, I noted, looked just the same as the one I'd come through on my way into this realm, as though the same tree existed in two worlds.

'The museum is kind of...'

'Upsetting? Yeah. That's war for you. Maybe you should come again another time and see some of the less depressing parts of our realm.'

'Maybe I will,' I said over my shoulder, as I joined the fast-moving queue going back through the door. I certainly should come again, if only to tell the fae queen what little I knew. Maybe the theft was connected to my impending travels, maybe not – but it felt like something she should know.

First, though, I was going to confront Laine and make him tell me *everything*.

∽

When I got to the Museum of Magical Artefacts, I rushed up to the fifth floor and stood panting in front of the Griffin.

'Michaelmas!' I cried, holding my stomach; a painful stitch was forming. People often warned you not to swim too soon after eating. What they should really warn about was not rushing back to work after witnessing the death (murder?) of a rabbit-like man.

The Griffin slid aside. 'Laine isn't up there,' he informed me in his deep, rumbling voice. 'If that's why you're using the password – and in such a rush, too.'

'Where is he?' I questioned.

'He ran out of here about twenty minutes ago, after a phone call from Ralph. I believe he has gone out to look for you.'

'Oh.' I stood on the spot, not really knowing what to do. I'd been so set on confronting Laine, and now that he wasn't here, it felt ever so anti-climactic. I'd rehearsed what I would ask, and how – even the tone of my voice had been planned down to the last inflection.

'I don't know what to do now,' I admitted, looking

helplessly at the Griffin. 'Do you know where he intends to look for me? Because if he goes and hassles my mother, that will *not* go well for him. She's far more ... shall we say *confident*? ... since she finally kicked Dad to the kerb.'

'I cannot be certain. However, I believe you told him you were spending your morning off having your hair done, so perhaps he is doing the rounds of the glamour salons.'

Oh, crap, I *had* told him that's what I was up to this morning. There were a lot of glamour salons in Warren Lane. He could be searching them for quite the while. And calling him was out of the question because, like me, Laine was one of those weirdos who didn't have a mobile phone.

'It's about time for elevenses, isn't it?' the Griffin remarked. 'Perhaps you should go and relax while you wait. Some of Fee's Calming Camomile tea would be a good idea, methinks – you look a tad stressed.'

Scratching my head, I said, 'Yeah. Yeah, you're right, Griff. I'll go and have a cup of tea.'

∽

WHEN I GOT TO THE STAFF ROOM, I FOUND FEE AND HUGO IN there together, having their morning break. Fee had plenty of time to take breaks these days, because Hugo had actually come good – he'd convinced his father to hire full-time help for the gift shop and café. He'd even wangled a pay raise for Fee, and he spent as much time as he could stopping by to chat with her during the day.

From what I could see, Fee had everything she'd ever wanted – respect, a decent wage, and Hugo's attention. But this morning, she didn't look happy about any of it. In fact, she looked gaunt, dull-eyed and drawn. I was suddenly reminded of the oven's concerns.

'Annie.' Hugo stared up with surprise as I entered the room. 'I didn't expect you in until after lunch. Didn't you enjoy your morning off?'

'It was fine,' I said. 'I'm just – there's something I forgot to tell Laine, so I thought I'd better come in, but he seems to have rushed off somewhere or other.'

'You sound as if you don't know where, which surprises me – I would have thought he kept you up to date on his every move,' Fee said, a little sullenly. 'Y'know, seeing as you two seem to live in each other's pockets.'

'We're just ... working on something for the museum together,' I told her. 'We'll be finished with it soon enough.' And when we were, I'd hopefully have Dora in my arms. She'd have a sweet and believable explanation for everything, and she would be the best and loveliest familiar a witch could ever want. Together, we'd begin planning how in Hecate's name I was going to get out from under Ralph's thumb. In my imagination she had some great suggestions.

'Oh *that's* what we're calling it these days, is it?' Hugo smirked. 'Working on something together indeed. They used to call it something else in my day.'

I didn't say anything to that. Ralph had come up with a fiendish plan as to how Laine and I would explain all of this time we were spending together. He thought we should tell people we were dating. I hadn't actually come out and said those words to anyone. But I hadn't come up with a better excuse either, so now ... now I just said nothing.

Fee gave me a suspicious stare. 'We could have done with your help at the restaurant last night, Annie. A bunch of witches turned up without reservations. They were having a hen night for one of them, and they were incredibly difficult. Drunk, the whole lot of them. And they tried to bring a stripper in.'

'I'm sorry about that,' I said. 'It's just–'

'Now, don't be so hard on Annie, Fee,' Hugo cut in. 'She can't be everywhere at once, can she? Anyway, I'm not sure why you're still moonlighting at the Hungry Hippy. Dad's given you a pretty decent pay hike, hasn't he?'

'Sure he has,' Fee acknowledged. 'And I'm very grateful for that, Hugo. I just ... I like cooking.'

Well, now *I* was the suspicious one. Sure, Fee liked cooking, but I *knew* she didn't like cooking steaks and burgers, which were always on the menu at the Hungry Hippy these days. She was lying, and I didn't know why. Her lie might be a decent segue, though.

'Well, I know you really like cooking,' I began. 'And the customers at the restaurant love you. But maybe you *are* stretching yourself a bit too thin. Mam would be sad to lose you, of course, but if you need a break...'

'I don't need a break,' she ground out. 'I'm perfectly fine.'

'Well, maybe I'll switch things around so I can join

you for a shift or two again. If things are as busy as you say, then–'

'Oh, don't bother!' she cried, interrupting me.

'Fee...' I recoiled a little. Things between us had begun badly, but over the weeks we'd become friends. Now, though, she was so peed off with me that it was kind of scary. 'Calm down, okay, I just...' I winced, wishing I could take the words back. Telling someone to calm down was about the worst thing you could say in an argument. 'I'm just worried about you, that's all. You look tired.'

'Oh, do I?' She crossed her arms, and I could hear a low growl at the back of her throat. 'Well, you're mistaken. I'm full of the joys of spring, me, and I can cope perfectly well with my two jobs, thank you very much. In fact, I coped *so* well without you last night that we got everything cleaned up nice and early and I found the time to make myself a lovely lentil loaf. It'll do me for days if I go easy on it, have it with lots of salad.' She smiled in a beatific way (translation: in a crazy manner). 'So much healthier than anything else on the menu – no offence to your menu, of course. But you know, the best way to keep the wolf away is not to feed it.'

Funny, because I was just thinking that the best way to *rile* a wolf was to starve her senseless and try to convince her she wasn't a werewolf at all. But what did I know? I certainly wasn't going to say as much, anyway, not when she had that hungry look in her eyes.

She got to her feet and began to make herself another cup of tea. While her back was turned away from us, I could hear her humming her abstinence song:

. . .

*'Nothing's as good for monsters as denial
Denial, denial, it's always the way to act
Nothing's as good for monsters as abstinence
Abstain, abstain, and forge a better path!'*

'WELL,' SAID HUGO,' LOOKING JUST AS BEMUSED AS I FELT. 'I'll leave you to it so, Fee. See you at lunch?'

She nodded, and carried on singing.

⁓

I THOUGHT THAT MY MOOD WAS ABOUT AS FLAT AS IT COULD BE, but when I got to my work area I realised: I was about to become a whole lot more deflated, and quick. Because there was Jake, working away at the bench next to mine, his deft hands moving quickly as he painted a tiny copy of one of the museum's more infamous pieces: the poisoned apple given to Snow White, with a perfect little bite taken out of it.

Experts were of mixed opinion as to whether it was the real apple, but one of Ralph's predecessors had preserved it anyway and put it on show, alongside a glass coffin and various dwarfen mining tools.

'Looks good,' I remarked as I began to set up for work. I might as well keep myself busy while I waited to confront Laine.

Jake grunted, then looked up. 'Oh. Yeah. Thanks.' He

worked away in silence for a while, fading further from my view, and it made my stomach hurt. Jake had been less and less visible by the day. I could only fully see him from time to time.

It hadn't been immediate. For a couple of days after Laine announced we'd be working together, Jake made a few more attempts to talk to me about ... well ... the possibility of us. Being Jake, it was always hard to know for *sure*, but it had certainly seemed like he was trying to ask me out. But I'd had to make excuses, each and every time, and now ... now he was focused on his work and nothing more.

I tried to concentrate on my own work, but I was finding it hard. Half of my brain was thinking about all of the things I wanted to say to Jake, while the other half was replaying Fee's abstinence song. I *hated* that song. It reminded me of the coven hymns my dad had forced me to sing as a child. Well, chocolate would never be evil, no matter what Dad's stupid lyrics might say, and Fee wasn't a monster, either. It bothered me that she thought she was.

And denial? That wasn't good for anyone. Fee couldn't truly deny what she really was, just like *I* couldn't deny I was nuts about Jake. It was as if my whole body hummed when he was around. Even now, in my misery, it was happening. And his smell ... good goddess, I wanted to sink my nose into his neck.

'So, Annie,' he said, so suddenly it made me jump. 'You might have seen the posters in our window.'

I swallowed down my surprise and looked at him. Just when I'd been thinking he was lost to me, his face was suddenly visible once more, and his eyes looked like great big pools of caramel, his freckles like tiny chocolate shavings. Oh my. Fearing I was about to salivate, I tore my eyes from his.

'You're talking about the art show you're having tonight?' I guessed. I'd seen the posters in the window at *Fuelling Art,* the café and art supply store he owned with his brother.

'I mean, you're probably busy with Laine, what with it being a Friday night.'

'I'm not,' I said, a little too quickly. 'I mean, we might have to work until eight or so, but the show starts at half past, doesn't it?' Not that I'd ogled the posters a thousand times or anything.

'Yeah, it's half eight it starts.' He hit me with a thoroughly mixed-up expression, half smile, half frown. 'Fee said she'll try her best to stop in, and Hugo said he'll be there. But ... when I was talking to Hugo about it, Laine overheard us and he said – he said you and he definitely had plans. So then, because I've tried to bring it up before and you've shut me down, I thought ... I thought maybe I should leave it.'

He faded a little, looking away from me. 'It's fine if you don't make it,' he went on. 'I mean, I'm not *that* freaked out that Alex is insisting on showing some of my work.' He faded even further, and resumed painting his miniature poisoned apple.

'Laine was mistaken,' I announced. 'I'll be there tonight, Jake. Count on it.' I spoke with absolute certainty. I didn't care what I had to do, how much I had to argue with Laine about it, but I *would* be there. I couldn't expect Jake to hang on and wait for me until I sorted out this Ralph business. I needed to show him that I cared. 'I do *not* have plans tonight. I don't know why Laine said we did.'

Jake grunted, then said, 'Well, he said you always have dinner together after work, actually. And breakfast before.'

We'd occasionally gorged on burgers or pizzas after a training session, but I wouldn't call it having dinner together. And our breakfasts? We went for exhausting runs, or had defence sessions, followed by a protein shake before getting on with even more training.

'Is um … is Karen going?' I tried to sound airy and nonchalant, but my heart was beating like a crazed drummer boy. The last time we'd spoken of Karen she'd been his *ex,* but I was so out of the loop these past few days that, for all I knew, they were now married with twins on the way.

'I haven't invited her,' he replied. 'I haven't seen her since – well, since that day you came over to see the place and she'd just turned up. She's been calling and stuff, but I've not been answering. She's left lots of messages, though.'

'Oh.' I sank into myself a little, wondering what she was saying in those messages, and whether she'd used a sexy and alluring voice. Probably. If she wanted Jake back (and let's face it, any sensible woman would) she'd pull out all the stops.

He turned on his stool and looked directly at me, one hundred percent present. 'She said that if I got back together with her, things would be different this time. She said she loves me.'

'Oh.' I was really hot with the wordplay today. In my defence, with all of Jake's attention on me it was hard to think straight. 'That's ... what do you think about that?'

'I don't know. If she'd said any of this even a few weeks ago, maybe I would have gone back to her like I always do. But now ... Annie, I – I'm kind of confused about exactly what's happening between you and Laine. I know you just said you don't have plans, but you're always together. Look, you can just tell me, because I'd rather know where I stand, and whether ... whether I should just bow out, y'know. So, these dinners and breakfasts you're having, are they ... are they couple-type meals, or friend-type meals?'

I stared back at him, wondering what the heck to say. This was *so* not fair. He was clearly still holding out for me, which was ... well, it was amazing. My feelings for him had only grown stronger by the day, and it was such a relief to know he hadn't given up on me. But whether he continued to hang on, or decided to give up, well ... it all hinged on the answers I was about to give him.

I couldn't tell him the specifics of the job, or my power. But I couldn't carry on as I'd been doing, either, with everyone believing Laine and I were an item while I just passively sat there, neither confirming nor denying. It was time to tell the truth – not the whole truth, and certainly not nothing *but* the truth – but ... some of the truth, anyway.

'Jake,' I began, wiping my palms on my jeans. 'First,

and I want to be absolutely clear with you on this, Laine and me, we are *not*–'

'There you are!' came Laine's voice, as he pushed his way into the warehouse. 'I've been looking for you everywhere. I need to talk to you, Annie.'

I sawed my jaw. He couldn't have picked a worse time to arrive if he'd been trying. 'Can't it wait?'

He glanced at Jake, then shook his head at me. 'Afraid not. It's super important.'

CHAPTER 5
RUSH JOB

Laine didn't say anything more to me. He simply marched ahead, making his way up to the fifth floor, assuming I'd follow. Well ... I *would* follow, but only so I could give him some very stern words once we got where we were going.

I moved slowly behind him, refusing to rush, knowing I'd need to keep my breath if I wanted to be at my most argumentative.

'Michaelmas,' he barked at the Griffin.

I didn't think he saw it, but the Griffin arched a brow before sliding aside, looking entirely unimpressed by Laine's manner.

Once we were both up in Ralph's office, Laine fixed me with a shrivelling glare. 'You need to get a phone, Annie. I had to reach you this morning, urgently. I've been rushing around all over the city looking for you.'

I drew myself up to my full height. 'My morning off's been scheduled for ages, Laine. Tell you what – you get a phone first, then I'll get one.'

His eyes glinted dangerously. 'You can't go out with him, you know.'

'What? Who?'

'You know very well who. Relationships don't work for people like us. How can they, when we can't tell anyone about our gifts? I mean ... you *could* tell him, technically speaking, but he'll forget it the second he walks out the door of the museum. And if you try to tell him again and again, the museum will just carry on forcing him to forget. Pretty soon, all of those memory adjustments will give him Swiss cheese for brains.'

'That can't be true. Can it?'

'Annie, you signed a contract with this museum, and it will abide by it. It will do *anything* necessary to keep your secret safe.'

'But ... you and Ralph and Hugo, you all get to know. There must be a way some other trusted members of staff can be let in on the secret. Jake wouldn't endanger me. And I don't think Fee would either, actually.' Sure, she'd looked awfully angry this morning, but I was convinced she could remedy her issues with a few pounds of rare meat.

'I *miss* them, Laine,' I went on. 'We were becoming friends, you know. Now they think I'm going out with you, because of all the time we're spending together. And it's really annoying them that I won't just come out and say: *"Yes, Laine and I are a couple."* They think I'm being weird and secretive.'

'Well, then you should just say: *"Yes, Laine and I are a couple."* Shouldn't you?'

I folded my arms. 'I'm not lying to them.'

'Fine. Let them carry on thinking you're being weird and secretive, then. It's no skin off my nose. I don't see why you fancy him, anyway. He's so wet.'

'Jake is not wet.'

'He's an absolute and utter drip, Annie. Afraid of his own shadow. Someone with a dangerous job like you've got, you need a real man by your side.'

'Oh yeah?' I cocked a brow. 'Pity I don't know any of those. Anyway, I thought you just said I *couldn't* date. I presume the embargo includes *real* men?'

He gritted his teeth. 'Why are you being such a smartarse with me today? You know what...' He shook his head. 'We've got too much work to do right now to worry about this. I was trying to track you down this morning because our job's been brought forward. We leave...' He checked his watch. '...in about half an hour.'

I looked from Laine to the mirror and back again. 'What? Why the sudden rush?'

'Apparently Ralph's just heard some news. There's been a robbery at the Museum of Never Again, and for some reason that means we've got to work fast.'

'Oh. Yeah, I wanted to talk to you about that, actually. I was there. I think it was something from the Prison Worlds Exhibition. It wasn't just a robbery, though. I think a guy called Mr Coneen was killed, too. And Laine, there was a tea set there that looked *very* like the sort of thing a Hatter and a March Hare might use for a party.' I didn't mention the connection to Dora, or to my dreams. 'Does that tea set have anything to do with our expedition? Because it's something from that exact exhibition that's been nicked. That's what Mr Coneen said before the other White Rabbit Guards escaped – maybe after one of them murdered him, to stop him talking. You need to tell me more about this job, Laine. Did Ralph have anything to do with what happened at that museum?'

He gave me a sharp look. 'You said you were getting your hair done, Annie. Why were you at the Museum of Never Again? You didn't tell anyone there about where we're going, did you?'

'No. And you didn't answer my question.'

'I mean, isn't it obvious that it has something to do with our expedition? There are some details I'm not certain on myself, but all that matters is that it's made Ralph all antsy and eager to move. If you weren't visiting that museum about anything to do with our job, then ... oh ...' His gaze settled on my locket. 'Ah. I get it. You thought the faery queen might be able to help you find out what's going on with *that*. You heard the rumour that she made it, I guess, and that she visits her museum regularly. What *is* going on with it, Annie? It's not still cursed, is it?'

'It's not still cursed,' I said. 'So what happens now?'

'Changing the subject, I see.'

'I'm learning from the master.'

He glowered, then he grunted. Finally, he said, 'You'd better de-neutralise the mirror while I go get what we need for our trip.'

'What are you getting, exactly? A portal key?'

He gave me an uncertain look. 'I ... yeah, I think so.'

'You *think* so?'

'I've also got to pick up the details for someone we have to meet up with the second we get inside.'

'Ralph's got a contact *in* there?' I shivered, as a dart of ice-cold fear shot through me. 'I don't like this, Laine. If you know more, you have to tell me right now. Because I swear, I'll just walk out of here, and I don't give a crap about the consequences.'

I must have looked deadly serious, because he sighed and said, 'Okay, okay, look ... I *don't* know about this Mr Coneen being killed, Annie, other than what you just told me. But Ralph has given me some extra info today. He said that we'll be entering Ciara's version of the *Through the Looking Glass* world, but we'll need to get to her version of Wonderland, and fast. That's where Ralph's contact comes in, because we'll need his help. And if we don't meet him at the specified time, well ... the worlds are connected, and we *could,* technically, make it to the Wonderland section of the world, but ... there's a very big chance that we'll get caught and become snacks for the Bandersnatch. So just make sure you de-neutralise the mirror, and have it ready for when I get back, okay, so we can be there at the right time.'

He left me standing there, my mouth open, as he walked out of the room.

'I'd like to de-neutralise *you*,' I grumbled, as I heard his steps fade away. 'And no, I don't know what I mean by that.'

~

As I moved to the cupboard and brought out the de-neutralising solution and a cloth, I heard a voice speaking. It was Athena, my favourite Grecian statuette. I'd recently told her she could speak freely with me as long as we were alone, or with Hugo. She didn't *want* to speak with Laine or Ralph present, so the instruction suited us both. It meant that she had no trouble keeping still as a statue whenever she needed to. She got ever so nervous if she was animated when Laine was in the room.

'Bad day, huh?' she said.

'The worst,' I agreed as I moved to the mirror and sprayed. The de-neutralising solution smelled even worse than the neutralising one. I'd had to de- and re-neutralise this mirror every night now for days. Laine said it was just practice so we could work quickly when the time came to go through. But if it was practice, then *he* wasn't doing any of it. He just stood there 'supervising' me the whole time.

Sometimes, while he 'supervised', he would look at me expectantly. I didn't know what he was expecting, exactly, but it was *something*. Inevitably his face would then fall into a look of disappointment (it was a look I knew well, having Windflower as a father) and he would begin to bark questions at me, asking me things that were none of his business, like who Dora was, and why I was willing to do this job just to help her.

Most of the time I would ignore him and carry on cleaning. But every now and then I would bark right back, telling him that if he wanted to know more about Dora, then he could blooming well tell *me* more about this job, first.

Actually, now that I thought about it, there was something unnatural, something rehearsed, about Laine's manner whenever he brought up the dormouse.

Maybe I was imagining it, but I didn't think so. Maybe Ralph had told him to ask me about her. But why? If Ralph was so certain that Dora was in need of saving, then he already knew far more about the dormouse than I did.

As I worked on the mirror today, I met Athena's eyes via our reflections. 'I don't want to go in there,' I told her. 'But I guess I'm going to, because it might be the only way I'll ever see Dora again.'

'Oh, I do hope you find her, Annie,' said Athena. 'I met her only briefly, but I liked her enormously.'

'Yeah, she has that effect on people. Although ... recent revelations are making me kind of scared that she might not be as sweet as she seems.'

'Oh, she is. I can tell. She's definitely not working for Queen Ciara – or, if she is, it's not willingly.'

'So, you could hear the conversations I've been having in this room with Laine?'

'I could hear. But thanks to your last instructions to me, I couldn't throttle him. That's a good thing, Annie, because goodness knows what Ralph would do with me if he found out I was sentient. You know he fancies you, right?'

My eyes grew round. 'Who, Ralph?'

'Not *Ralph*. Laine. I catch him looking at you sometimes, when the two of you are up here and he's testing you on your knowledge of *Alice*. But...'

'But what?'

'I don't know, Annie.' Her tone was uneasy. 'Sometimes he looks at you lustfully, but sometimes there's ... something else in his gaze. Something I can't quite place.' She shrugged her stone shoulders. 'Perhaps it's just that he's annoyed with you. You do give him a lot of back talk.'

'Yeah, well, he's not the boss of me,' I muttered. 'And if he wants my respect, he has to earn it.'

'He *did* rush to your aid when you were battling the murderous mummy. Granted, you were quite capable of sorting the situation out for yourself, but at least he tried.'

'I know,' I said with a sigh. 'And I was really glad he tried to come through for me that day – he totally went against Ralph's instructions. But there are things he's not telling me about this job. Things I *know* he knows. He didn't look remotely surprised when I told him about the tea set, and he didn't even flinch when I mentioned the murder.'

I thought about Mr Coneen, lying there, clearly dead. He'd been rude to me, but now I understood why: he'd had some very important things to discuss with his queen. Maybe if I'd left the museum just a second or two earlier, like he clearly wanted me to, he'd still be alive. 'Athena, you seem to know everything about everything. Have you ever heard of a rabbit shifter?'

'A supernatural who can transform into a rabbit, you mean?' She brought a hand to her chin, tapping thoughtfully with her fingers. 'I've seen some hares in my time, but I've never met a rabbit shifter, personally. However, there have to be *some*. There's every other kind of shifter, isn't there? And the Púca, of course, are exceptionally adept at becoming anything they wish, though they tend to stick to becoming horses and goats, for the most part.

Some witches, too, are gifted at transformational spells. Why? Do you think you met a rabbit shifter?'

'The White Rabbit Guard,' I said. 'They don't *look* like rabbits, not exactly. But they hop and they twitch and they have pink eyes and they're just generally kind of ... rabbity. Anyway, the craziness at the Museum of Never Again this morning, it has *something* to do with this job. What if Ralph's behind it, and Laine knows all about it, and he's just fine and dandy with working for a murderer?'

'Ralph is many things, Annie. But I don't think he's a killer.'

'Maybe.' I wasn't convinced. 'But Athena, what if I go in there with Laine, and ... and I don't come out?'

'You'll come out, Annie. I'm certain of it.'

CHAPTER 6
THROUGH THE LOOKING GLASS

I carried on working, frowning at the mirror, not feeling even a little bit as certain as Athena seemed to be. I also felt like my senses were going a little screwy, because I was sure I could hear voices in there. And I thought I could see something, too – the image was blurred, as though it was at the bottom of a deep pool of water, but it appeared to be whiskery and twitchy. Could it be those White Rabbit Guard guys? Suspicious as I was of them after this morning, I felt the strongest urge to jump on through and see what they were up to.

I took a step back from the mirror. I couldn't just leap in there. Could I? I shook my head and muttered, 'Nah, don't be an eejit, Annie.'

Something really was going on with me today, because I was *not* the kind to take leaps into the unknown. I was the kind who loved to read about adventures, but I'd always been far too terrified to pursue any of my own. I'd hated every sticky situation Ralph had placed me in since coming to work here, and I did *not* want to find myself in another.

And yet ... *thoughts* kept coming into my mind. Thoughts like: just do it, Annie, just jump through that mirror. Thoughts like: Dora is in there, and she needs you.

These stupid thoughts were fudge-all use to me. It wasn't as if I *could* just jump through that mirror. We needed a portal key, according to Laine – though he'd seemed suddenly uncertain of that during our most recent chat, which was kind of weird.

Ignoring all logic, I found myself focusing harder on the mirror. The whiskery, twitchy faces seemed to grow less blurry, as if they were drawing closer to me. I could hear them speaking now, their words growing clearer. One said, 'Annie hasn't come in yet,' while another replied, 'She'll be ever so late for croquet. Queen Ciara will be...' Well, I didn't know *what* she'd be, because they began to draw further away again. They sounded worried, though.

My curiosity grew and grew, until it was all I could think of. Dora *was* in there, I felt it, like a tugging sensation somewhere inside me, an invisible cord running between us. I had to go in. I had to. I reached out, my hand touching the mirror. It felt like ... like putting my hands into water, only the water was somehow not wet.

I suddenly heard more voices, only these ones were coming from outside the office. I jerked away from the mirror again. It was Jake and Fee, coming up the tower stairs. They appeared in the doorway mid-bicker, Fee brushing Jake's hand from her arm and saying, 'I'm going in, Jake!' while Jake said, 'We can't just barge into Ralph's office, Fee!'

I gave them both a small (and probably guilty) smile. 'Well, you're here now,' I said. 'Um ... how *did* you get up here, out of curiosity?'

Fee lifted her chin and said, 'The Griffin was open, which in my mind makes it perfectly acceptable. Jake wasn't sure about it, bless him, but seeing as Laine's just left the building in an awful hurry – looked like he was worried, so he did – *I* thought it might be the only chance we get to talk to you in private. What's going on here, Annie? What are you and Laine really up to? And why did he look like he was about to come face-to-face with swift and sudden death just now?'

I did my best to meet her eyes. 'You have an amazing imagination. He's just gone out to grab some food, as far as I know. Although if he's heading to the Byrne and Byrne supermarket around the corner, he might feel deathly sick when he sees the prices.'

Fee let out a sarcastic, 'Aha ha ha,' and added, 'You're such a bad liar.'

'So this is your secret job?' Jake looked at me in confusion. 'Ralph's got you cleaning mirrors?'

'It's ... it's a special solution, because the mirrors are magical. Pretty much everything in here is.'

Hugo suddenly appeared behind them, panting, straightening his bowtie and brushing back his curly hair. 'Yes, yes that's it,' he said, once he'd caught his breath. 'It's just as Annie says. The artefacts in here need specialist care. My father likes Annie and Laine to do it, as they're used to dealing with such things, don't you know.'

I tossed Hugo a quizzical glance. As far as I knew, he had no idea what Laine and I were working on – Laine had said I wasn't to talk to him about it – and yet he was covering for us. Maybe he *did* know something, or at least suspect.

'Oh, sure, *that's* what Annie's been up to all week. Specialist care of Ralph's ever so important artefacts.' Fee narrowed her eyes. 'And I eat steak tartare for breakfast, lunch and dinner.' She wiped away a sudden spot of saliva and went on. 'Look, there's something going on in this museum. I sense it, Hugo, and I'm getting really peed off with the way you keep lying to me.'

'I'm not lying,' he squeaked, his cheeks turning purple.

'You are, though, I know you are, because I know you, Hugo, through and through. Your dad was way too quick to agree to my pay raise when you asked him, *and* he let you hire assistants for me again. Plus, he bought Jake all of that new equipment for souvenir-making, *and* he's given him an extra day off each week so he can spend time helping Alex at Fuelling Art. I'm guessing he thinks if he keeps us happy we'll ask no questions – he reckons we won't want to rock the broom. Well, I don't care for riding brooms, so I'll happily rock them, because something off is happening here. I feel it in my bones. And it's got something to do with why Annie and Laine are spending all of this time together.'

'They're clearly dating!' Hugo insisted. 'I've told you already.'

Oh, he definitely knew what was going on. With a lie like that, there was no doubting it. Plus, he was doing his best not to look Fee in the eye. He pulled a monocle out of a little purse and concentrated very hard on polishing it.

'They're not dating,' Fee said with vehemence. 'It's absolutely impossible that they're dating. Isn't it, Jake?'

Jake gave her a sad little shrug. 'I don't know about *impossible.*'

'Exactly.' Hugo clapped Jake on the back. 'My man here knows what I'm talking about. It might seem impossible to you, Fee, that Annie would be dating Laine. But surely, working in this museum has made you believe in the impossible. Why, sometimes I've believed as many as six impossible things before breakfast.'

My eyes snapped to Hugo's. 'Why did you say that?'

'Say what?'

'That's – that's from *Through the Looking Glass.* The White Queen says *exactly* what you just said, Hugo. She tells Alice that she tries to believe six impossible things before breakfast.'

'Does she?' Hugo shrugged and affixed his monocle to his eye. 'Never read it. Father doesn't like me to read books about humans going where they oughtn't. The point is, Annie and Laine are a perfect match, Fee, and that's all there is to it.'

'Perfect match!' Fee spat. 'As *if.* Annie doesn't fancy Laine in the slightest. I'd smell it if she did. Laine isn't her type.' She cast a brief glance at Jake and then looked at me again. 'Is he, Annie?'

'It ... he ...' Crap. One of these days, I'd get better at

lying to Fee's face. Right now, I was too busy freaking out about the power of her nose. I would never be able to keep a secret from this woman. Not unless I could find a spell to render her anosmic.

As I looked pleadingly at Hugo, waiting for him to spring to my aid again, I noticed that his face had paled, and that he was staring at the mirror in an absolute daze. And ... why were his eyes suddenly spinning?

As I peered closer, I realised that his eyes *weren't* spinning. They were simply reflecting what he was looking upon – the mirror, at its very centre, *that* was what was spinning, and quickly. It was hypnotic, scary, and a little bit sickening. My stomach churned as I looked upon it. Now I understood why Hugo was quoting a book he'd never read. Because that world was calling to him, the same way it was calling to me. And Laine might have insisted we needed a key, but right now I was afraid he might be wrong.

The mirror's power was obvious to me now, even though it had been absent before. I could feel its desires – feel that it *wanted* me to touch it again. And I really, really wanted to obey.

'You guys need to leave,' I said. 'It – I've got a lot of work to do.'

'Fine,' Fee agreed. 'No point in staying here anyway, is there – not while you insist on wallowing in your rotten web of lies.'

Ignoring the barb, I put my hands on Hugo, trying to move him aside. He was surprisingly sturdy, his gaze remaining steady on the looking glass.

Fee frowned at him and said, 'Snap out of it, Hugo. You're freaking me out.'

Hugo didn't answer. He was still staring, entranced, at the swirling mirror.

'Jake.' Fee gulped. 'Hugo's being *really* weird. And ... can you smell some sort of smoke?'

Jake paid no attention to her, but not because he was entranced by the mirror. He was staring, instead, at the ceiling. As I followed his eyes I froze in terror, gawking at the horror above me: an enormous spider, getting ready to pounce. It was a Loony Lunger, and it was three times bigger than the last one I'd seen.

'Look out, Annie!' Jake cried suddenly, pushing me out of the way.

The last time Jake saved me from a spider had been oddly enjoyable – we'd lain on the ground together, and I'd revelled in his paint and turpentine smell. This time was far less intimate, because in his panic, Jake was a little overenthusiastic.

As he pushed me, I fell against Fee, who fell against Hugo – and somehow, in a great big clumsy mess of limbs and terror, all four of us fell against the swirling mirror, and were sucked inside.

CHAPTER 7
FRUMIOUS JAWS

I'd already been through an interdimensional portal today, if you counted the door to the fae realm. But it had been nothing like this. This ... well, this was like going through a spin-cycle at hyper-speed. I felt like I was being pulled and pushed in a thousand different directions – and if my insides *weren't* mixed up with my outsides by the time this was over, then I would at least have developed some wobbling jowls.

The four of us struggled to stay together, clutching onto whatever we could, whenever we could (mental purges would be required later on), all of us shouting various versions of 'What the frick?' as we were tumbled and tussled about.

At one point close to the beginning, while Hugo was in danger of coming loose from the rest of us, he tried to reach for my waist, but when he did so, I felt his hand go to my back pocket and grab at my wand instead. His eyes met mine as he tried to hand it back, but the vortex spun it right out from his grip.

When I finally tumbled to the ground, tangled up with the others, it was only shock that stopped me from puking. We were still in Ralph's office, and the mirror I *thought* we'd just travelled through ... it wasn't swirling anymore.

'What happened?' Fee asked, staring all around her. 'I thought we just went through some sort of ... I don't know. Like ... the mirror swallowed us. Then spun us around like a bunch of clothes in a dryer before spitting us out again.' She scratched her head. 'I mean, I clearly imagined it, because we're still here in Ralph's office.' Sniffing, she added, 'I still smell smoke, though.'

'I smell it too,' I murmured, looking up into Jake's eyes. I also smelled the citrussy scent of his soap mixing in with his usual work smells, but I didn't think mentioning it would help matters. 'It's an unusual kind of smoke, though. Strong, but ... exotic?'

Jake groaned, disentangled himself from the rest of us, and sat up. 'This is wild. You think it was a portal mirror? I mean, it wouldn't be surprising, given we work in the Museum of Magical Artefacts, right?'

Hugo was very carefully *not* looking at any of us as he replied: 'Portal mirror? No. I think maybe you didn't get Annie away from the Looney Lunger in time, Jake. I think maybe you got bit too, Fee, if you think you got swallowed by a mirror.'

'You don't think we got swallowed by a mirror?' Jake questioned, looking curiously at Hugo. 'Because I'm certain that *I* got swallowed by a mirror.'

'You should be – because we did get swallowed by a mirror,' I stated. It seemed silly to lie, seeing as we'd all just experienced the exact same thing.

I gazed around the room. Now that I was over my initial shock, I saw that it didn't look *quite* the same. Portraits were backwards, titles on book spines were written in gobbledygook. 'No, it's not gobbledygook – it's mirror writing,' I murmured, rushing to one of the books and picking it up. Opening it, I found the same backwards-written poem Alice had found when she went through the mirror: Jabberwocky.

Next, I went to the window. Normally, through Ralph's window I would see the city stretching out before me, both human parts and supernatural; I would see the Wyrd Court tower, and the wonky structure of Crooked College.

Now, though, I didn't see any of that. The world outside this window was an altogether different one. It seemed to be twilight out there, but a hazy twilight with a reddish-orange tint. Something about the air quality looked menacing.

There was a large garden below us, with flowers which seemed to be chatting and shrieking – one of them appeared to be waving up at me. To one side of the garden there was a forest so large I couldn't see the end of it, and to the other side was a great stretch of grass mowed in a checkerboard fashion. 'Or a giant chess board,' I muttered.

'Why are you muttering and mumbling to yourself?' Fee complained, standing up and joining me at the window. 'Holy werewolf balls!'

'I echo that sentiment,' said Jake, standing next to her. 'We *are* in another world.'

As Hugo stumbled over to us, he shook his head and said, 'Oh dear, oh dear, we shouldn't be here. My father will be so angry with me. We have to go back. Annie, Jake, Fee – come on!'

He grabbed hold of Fee and Jake, and though he tried to yank them over to the mirror, they shook themselves out of his grasp.

He gritted his teeth and said, 'Come on, guys. This is – this isn't happening, okay? You're not seeing what you think you are. The spider must've bitten all of you. A mass hallucination, that's what's happening here. We're in the same place we were when you all think we left it, so whatever you felt just now must be your imagination.'

Fee gave him a look of disgust and said, 'Ever see a film called *Gaslight*, Hugo?'

'I have not. But I'm not such a fuddy duddy that I can't understand a modern reference, Fee. And I am not *gaslighting* you,' he insisted. 'Why do women always think men are gaslighting them? Sometimes ... sometimes it's better not to know everything, okay? Sometimes you should just trust that I have your best interests at heart, and that whatever little white lies I might tell you are for your own good.'

'You need to quit while you're behind, Hugo,' Jake suggested.

'Fine,' said Hugo with a huff. 'I admit it – we're in another world, okay? Are you happy now? Because you wouldn't be if you knew what *I* know. We shouldn't be here, and I'm sure Annie would agree with me on that.'

I gave him a slit-eyed stare. He *did* know everything about this job, the sly little bugger. 'I guess he's not wrong – this isn't a place we should be,' I said.

'Exactly,' he said smugly. 'So we need to get out of here. Right now.' As he spoke, he approached the mirror and poked at it. 'Annie, what's wrong with this thing? It feels solid, and it doesn't look all swirly anymore. I overheard Laine and Dad talking about a portal key. Can you use it to get us back?'

'Well, no, because I don't *have* the key,' I told him. 'Laine was going off to get it. At least ... I think he was.'

'What?' His eyes were filled with confusion. 'That's impossible. We're *here,* aren't we? How could that be possible, without a portal key?'

'Why are you asking me when you obviously know more than *I* do?' I snapped as I joined him at the mirror. 'I have no idea how we got here, okay?'

I knew something, though – in that same way I often knew so many things I shouldn't know about magical objects – I was certain we were stuck here. But, because I'm a glass half full sort of person, I decided to ignore my certainty and find a way out. I touched my hand against the mirror and discovered that Hugo wasn't *quite* right. It was solid, in a way, but it was also sort of bouncy, as if it was repelling my touch. When I tried to press harder, it pushed me away and I landed on my rear.

Jake helped me up and asked, 'Are you all right, Annie?'

'I'm really not,' I replied, feeling a little thrill while his hand was in mine – followed by a sinking sense of disappointment as he quickly let go. 'I don't understand any of this. I don't know why we're here and I don't know how to get out and ... just ... just give me a minute, okay?'

I reached into my back pocket for my wand, hoping I could do *something* with it (I had no idea what that something might be), but then I remembered: it wasn't there anymore. Hugo had lost it somewhere amongst all the spinning. I got on my knees and scoured the office floor, hoping with all my might that it had somehow made its way through with us, but it was nowhere to be found.

'What are we looking for?' asked Jake, as he and Fee joined me on the floor.

'My wand.'

'Will it help us?' Fee asked.

I bit my bottom lip. 'I don't know. Maybe.' I sighed and straightened up. 'It's not here, so I guess it doesn't matter either way. I'm so sorry guys, but I really do think we're stuck in this place.'

Hugo shook his head. 'No, no, I refuse to accept that. We'll try teleportation.' He clicked his fingers, and remained in exactly the same spot. 'That's funny...'

'There's nothing funny about any of this,' said Fee.

'No, I meant funny *strange* not funny as in *let's all chortle together*,' Hugo explained. 'I can't even feel my magic. Not the slightest tingle. I'm going to try something else.' He pointed at Jake and muttered some words. 'See? I've just tried to shrink Jake and nothing.'

'Huh.' Jake wiggled his finger, trying various spells that I absolutely recognised, because I'm ever so good at magic (ahem). 'My power's on the fritz, too.'

Fee pulled out her wand and tried a few things. 'It's not working,' she said with a grunt of irritation. 'This is my college wand. It's got magic of its own, so even if you bunch of witches have lost your innate magic, I should be able to do *something* with this. But ... nada.'

'Oh, sod it, anyway!' I cried. 'Laine didn't say anything about magic not working here. What was the bloody point in him training me in all of those defensive spells if I can't use any of them?'

'But where exactly is *here*, Annie?' Fee questioned.

Before I could reply, Hugo dragged me into a corner. 'We can't tell them that, Annie. Let's you and I talk about this, decide the best way ahead. We need to find *some* way to get out of here before Dad finds out what's happened, so–'

'Hugo, we could be in here for days before he knows we're gone,' I interrupted. 'Time passes differently in here. Anyway, there's no point in you and I making some plan in the corner like whispering idiots, is there? Fee can probably hear every word we're saying.'

'Yes,' said Fee. 'I can.'

Hugo coughed uncomfortably and looked at his shoes. 'Right. Yes. Well ... it's like this ... it's...'

'It's *like* we've come through a portal to another world, a place which you're too much of a chicken to name,' said Fee. 'And we've got here by some weird twist of fate, right before Annie and Laine were due to come here on a job together, hunting down some trinket for your dad. Because I'm absolutely certain that work obligations are the *only* way that Annie would agree to spend that much time with Laine. I guess Ralph should have factored Loony Lungers into his plans, shouldn't he?'

I smiled at her. 'Sometimes I think you're just about the cleverest woman I know. But if you figured out that much, why did you keep hassling me?'

'Because. You're supposed to be my friend, and you won't trust me with this. Maybe – maybe you don't see me as a friend the way I see you. Maybe I'm just some joke to you. Some werewolf who's deluded herself that she can be reformed.'

'You're not a joke to me, Fee. I wasn't allowed to talk about this particular job. I–'

I broke off, wishing I could say more. But even if I did, the moment we got back – *if* we got back – then the museum would make her forget. I couldn't bear the thought of telling her everything only to have it whipped out of her mind again. What if there really *was* such thing as a Swiss-cheese brain?

Feeling incredibly conflicted, I gave her as much honesty as I could for now, as I said, 'Look, I don't even know what I'm supposed to find in this place, and I'm peed off and embarrassed that Ralph keeps putting me in these situations. I wish I could have talked to you about it, but...'

She rushed over to me, throwing her arms around me and drawing me into one of her super-strong hugs. 'Oh, I'm sorry, Annie. I shouldn't have been so hard on you. Not when I know just as well as you do what Ralph is like.' She pulled away to glare at Hugo. 'Your dad's a pig. You know that, don't you? Of course you do, because he's had you lying for him, right? You outright told me you thought Annie and Laine were together.'

While Hugo's mouth opened and closed (he was sure to think of a comeback eventually), Jake shot me a cautious smile and said, 'Look, I'm a natural pessimist, so I'm afraid I need you to put it for me as plainly as possible. You're really *not* dating Laine? Not even a little bit?'

'Not even an infinitesimal amount,' I said, looking him in the eye. 'Fee is right, Jake. Ralph's forced me to spend all of this time with Laine, so Laine could train me to come in here with him. But now ... here we all are, without him, and I really have no idea what it is Ralph wants in this world.'

'But Hugo knows,' said Fee. 'Don't you, Hugo? I can see how much you're squirming. You know a lot more about this than poor Annie does. What did Ralph tell you?'

'Nothing,' he said, sounding completely truthful. 'He told me Annie and Laine were doing something top-secret, and if anyone started asking questions, I was to make it seem like they were dating. That's really all he told me.'

'Fine. Maybe he didn't *tell* you – but you discovered something about it through other means, didn't you?' she guessed. 'I know you, Hugo – you're naturally nosy.'

'No I'm not! But ... I am naturally curious, so I *might* have put earwigging spells on Dad's phone and in his office, and occasionally listened at keyholes or down chimneys–' He broke off, his nose wrinkling in bafflement. 'Why would I listen down a *chimney*? Why did I say that?'

'It's another *Alice* reference,' I informed him. 'You know – from those books you said your dad wouldn't let you read. I'm getting the feeling we'll all be making a lot of those, whether we know what they mean or not. And no one cares if you're the nosy sort, Hugo. In any case, Laine's been known to listen in on *your* supposedly private conversations once in a while.'

'How dare he! Why, that low-down cur!'

'Seriously?' I quirked a brow. 'It's natural curiosity when you do it, but Laine's a cur for doing the same thing?'

Hugo had the good grace to grow flushed. 'Point taken. All right, look, Laine and Dad were being very cagey in their conversations. All I could really gather is that Laine wasn't happy about coming here – he said it was too dangerous even for him on his own, let alone taking Annie along. Father insisted Annie would help matters, not hinder them. He told Laine that he wanted you both to do whatever you need to do in here in order to get him some teapot. It's got playing card symbols painted on it. It's part of some mismatched set, but the teapot is the bit he really wants.'

My heart began to pound. 'That teapot. That bloody *teapot*. What does he want it for?'

'Laine asked that question,' said Hugo. 'Father declined to answer.'

I took some deep breaths as I tried to calm myself down. 'Hugo, I saw that teapot – or a fake of it, probably – with my own eyes this morning, at the Museum of

Never Again. Mr Coneen, one of the guards, he got killed right after he pointed to the display and told the fae queen that the entire tea set was a fake – the real stuff had supposedly already been stolen. Does your dad know anything about how that happened, by any chance? Because if he does, if he had *anything* to do with it, then that's the last straw for me.'

Hugo stared at me, a wounded look in his eyes. 'You went to another museum?'

I stared right back. 'That's what you're choosing to focus on right now?'

He cleared his throat. 'Yes, I'm sorry, it's terrible about Mr Coneen. May the goddess succour his soul. Look, Annie, I swear to you, I may have heard the word "teapot" mentioned, but I know nothing about any robbery or murder.'

I wanted to believe him, I really did, because I liked him so much despite, well, everything. 'Fine,' I said. 'Whatever. Well, as we're all stuck here, then I'll tell you what little *I* know about this place. This is a prison world.'

'A prison world?' Fee gaped at me. 'Those places are meant to trap the worst prisoners, right? The ones so dastardly that they can't be kept safely at Witchfield. I'm kind of afraid to ask this, but ... did Ralph or Laine bother to tell you whose prison it is?'

'Yeah, Laine told me, but you're not going to like it,' I said with a sigh. 'A person called Ciara is trapped here – only *she* calls herself the Queen of Minds. She was obsessed with Lewis Carroll's works, especially *Alice's Adventures in Wonderland* and *Through the Looking Glass*.

She created this world herself, before she was sealed in here. I think Laine said it's called Wonkyland or Wonky Wonderland, or variations on the same. And from what I've seen outside, we've landed in the part of the world based on the second *Alice* book. Queen Ciara, she um ...' My voice lowered and shook. 'She's an evil mind-controlling vampire who liked to lure seven-year-old girls into this realm.'

I took in a shuddering breath, and carried on. 'And now ... well, you guys are somehow in here with me. And like you no doubt overheard me say to Hugo, time moves differently in here, so we could be gone for days before Laine even thinks of trying to come after us.'

Fee rushed to the easy chair and sat down. 'I feel faint. I know you've just told us a lot, but all I can focus on is "prison world". Oh, and the bit where she liked to lure seven-year-olds. Why seven-year-olds?'

'Alice was seven,' Jake said. 'In *Through the Looking Glass* she tells the White Queen she's "seven and a half exactly". Anyone obsessed with those books would want their Alices stuck at the right age, I guess.' He shuddered. 'So does that mean there's a bunch of creepy little vampire girls in here?'

I couldn't answer that question, not yet, because I was too busy smiling. 'You've read *Alice*?'

His face went red. 'I saw the books in your bag. I'd always meant to read them, so I got them. I had a quick glance last night, curled up on the couch with Wim.'

My heart grew warm, and I was filled with a sense of *wanting*. Wim was Jake's gorgeous familiar, an Old English Sheepdog. Thoughts of being curled up with the two of them, spending our evenings reading together, rushed into mind. Dora would be with us, snoozing in her teacup. Wim might get a little bored of reading and watch some tennis instead, and Jake and I would inch closer together, laughing at our familiars for a moment before returning to our books. Oh, I wanted that so, so much.

Fee stood up and waved her hand in my face. 'Um, Annie, could you come back from whatever dreamland you're in, please? You never answered Jake's question. Are we in a world filled with creepy seven-year-old vampire girls or what?'

I forced away my smile, and my lovely daydream, and said, 'No, thankfully. Anyone she kidnapped, they were evacuated before the world was sealed. But ... Ciara's not alone in here. There are a bunch of her cohorts imprisoned here, too.'

'Evil cohorts?' Fee asked, her voice shaking.

'I...' I paused, thinking about the fact that Dora could be in here. 'Maybe there'll be some who are helpful. Hopefully. Laine said we'd meet up with a contact, and that they'd help us get from where we've landed, and over to the Wonderland section of the world. We need to get there fast, apparently, otherwise, we could get um...' I lowered my voice and rushed out the rest. '...we could get eaten by something called the Bandersnatch.'

Fee's eyes darted all around, and I could see the yellow in her eyes begin to glow. 'What's a Bandersnatch when it's at home?'

'Characters in *Through the Looking Glass* mention it, but don't really describe it much, other than suggesting it's fast,' I told her. 'But in another piece by Lewis Carroll, we're told it's got *frumious* jaws. Please don't ask me what that means, because I have no idea.'

'It means a cross between fuming and furious,' Hugo supplied. 'Obviously.'

'Obviously,' I muttered, looking darkly at Hugo.

Fee let out a long, loud groan, and kicked the desk.

'Hey, watch it,' said Hugo.

'Why?' she roared. 'It's not like it's actually your dad's, is it? It's some stupid doppelganger of your dad's desk, in a world created by a psycho vampire!'

Hanging her head, she calmed herself down and said, 'I'm sorry, Hugo. I know I shouldn't have shouted at you, even if you *have* been a bit of a prat about all this. I know I'm being extra moody today, I do. But I'm – I'm just so hungry and tired.' She began to open drawers and cupboards, her stomach growling loudly. 'And there's nothing to *eat* in here! We have to get home, guys, we have to. I need some food, and I have an abstinence meeting at seven tonight that I can't miss. I – I just can't.'

Given how much she was shaking, I agreed with her. She looked like a woman in withdrawal. What were they doing to her at those meetings? It couldn't just be sing-songs, could it? Not when she was behaving so unlike herself. At least we were nowhere near full moon, otherwise I might fear she was about to wolf out.

Jake patted her shoulder gently. He'd remained surprisingly present since our arrival here. 'You'll be okay, Fee. We'll find something to eat, and we'll figure it out together, all of us, okay? I mean, Annie and I, we know all about the books, and those books are like dreams. Like *Alice's* dreams. I think we can get to anywhere we want, if we just want it enough. We can start with the flowers outside. They could be the contact Ralph was on about, couldn't they? I mean, they'll probably throw a lot of puns about barking trees our way, but maybe they'll give us some actual information too. And if that's not helpful, then we already know where the teapot is most likely to be – the tea party at the March Hare's house.'

'You've had more than just a quick glance, haven't you?' I said, giving him a big, dopey grin.

His lips twitched into a smile even bigger than mine. 'Alex and Wim teased me mercilessly, saying I was only reading it because I like you. And you should have heard Alex's familiar. She gives a new and more terrifying meaning to the word *sarcasm*. I guess maybe you'll meet her tonight.'

'I guess maybe I will,' I said, twiddling my hair between my fingers. I knew it was hardly the time for flirting, but I couldn't help myself.

Her lips wobbling, Fee let out an irritable grunt and said, 'When the two of you find a minute to stop making googly eyes, could you maybe clarify something for me? Are you actually suggesting that w*e* go out there and try to be treasure hunters?'

'Well, we have to, don't we?' said Hugo in a matter-of-fact voice. 'If we stay here, we'll be eaten by the Bandersnatch.'

Fee glanced out the window and then shook her head. 'It can hardly get into this office, can it? We should just – just barricade ourselves in and wait for Laine.'

Jake snorted. 'We don't need Laine to rescue us. Anyway, we need to get you some food.'

Fee looked pleadingly at me. 'Annie, you agree with me, don't you? It's better to stay in here and hide from the Bandersnatch rather than go out there and get eaten by it, right?'

'Well, I ... I *want* to agree with you, because I really don't want us to be on the outs again,' I said. 'But I think that right now, I should be honest so ... no, I don't want to stay in here, because I don't think pushing some furniture against a door is going to keep out the Bandersnatch.'

'Exactly,' Hugo put in. 'Think about it, Fee – it's got frumious jaws. *Frumious.*'

'Well, anyway,' I said. 'That's what I think. Plus, Jake's right – we need to find you some food. And also ...' I hesitated, wondering whether to tell them this part. 'Well ... Ralph said coming into this world was the only way I could save Dora. He didn't specifically say she was *in* here, but I ... I get the impression from Laine that she might be, so ...' I let my words trail off. I could tell them more, like the fact that I'd dreamt about her being here, in the teapot, but seeing as my dream could be connected to my gift, it was just another thing Fee and Jake might be forced to forget.

'You think *Dora* is in here?' Hugo stared at me in shock.

'Who's Dora?' Jake asked.

'Annie's familiar,' replied Fee with a gasp. 'At least, Dora says she is, only she keeps disappearing. She's the cutest little dormouse, but I had no idea she was magical until Annie told me so. Until then, any time I met Dora in the storeroom I'd chatter away to her, having no idea she understood every word. But ... how could she be here?' She fixed her eyes on Hugo.

'I don't know,' he said. 'Honestly, I don't.'

'I have to be straight with you,' I went on. 'Ralph said she was in trouble, but even the thought that she might be in here is kind of terrifying to me, because ... well ...'

'Because only Queen Ciara's evil cohorts are trapped in here with her,' Fee guessed.

'Yeah,' I agreed with a sigh. 'Because of that. So I'm going to go out there regardless of what you think. It might not be wise, but I – I care about her. I want to find her. I want to bring her home. And if she turns out to be evil, well ... I'll just have to cross that bridge if I come to it.'

Fee drew herself tall. 'That bridge doesn't exist, Annie. I have a nose for these things, and I'm telling you – that little dormouse is about the sweetest creature I've ever met.' She stomped to the office door. 'Well, what are you all waiting for? We need to get out there, fast. We've got a dormouse to save.'

CHAPTER 8
BY A WHISKER

Getting out into the garden was a whole lot harder than it sounded. Firstly, we had to get over the fact that outside the mirror-version of Ralph's office, nothing else was even remotely like the museum's central tower. There was an old-fashioned hallway and an elegant staircase with a door at the foot of it, and nothing else. I suppose I should have expected it, but it left me feeling weak at the knees – inside the office things had been familiar, if a bit backwards. Now, we were truly stepping into the unknown.

Although we weren't really *stepping,* because we didn't so much walk downstairs as we sort of ... floated. It might have been kind of fun if you didn't mind feeling like you were stuck inside a dream, but I *did* mind it. Even my own movements felt out of my control.

Once we got downstairs, we had trouble making it much further than that. We could open the door easily enough, but every time we tried to step outside, we found ourselves back at the top of the staircase. No matter how unpleasant it was, we attempted the journey again and again, because what else could we do? Fee was getting hungrier (and angrier), so being trapped inside with her was almost as dicey a prospect as facing the Bandersnatch.

It was probably the twentieth attempt (we'd stopped counting after a while), when I got angry and snarled, 'Well, Alice did it, so we're going to do it too. Let us out there. Now.'

I guess my current demeanour was just as scary as Fee's, because the doorway acquiesced, and we finally crossed the threshold.

When we emerged into the hazy, red-orange twilight, I began to wonder if outside really *was* a better prospect. The air felt so heavy, it was a struggle to breathe it in. And it didn't smell like normal air, either. It smelled sharp and unpleasant. It had a taste to it, too, but it wasn't a taste I'd experienced before. It was sort of ... muddy.

Fee shivered and stared upwards. Following her gaze, I saw something I didn't want to see. Far up there, beyond the haze, a silvery orb shone in the sky.

'It's full,' she said worriedly. 'How is it full? There wasn't a full moon back home.' She balled her fists. 'But it'll be fine. I don't need my No-Turn potion. My abstinence leader has taught me that turning is just ... it's mind over matter. It's *my* body, and I can make it do exactly as I want it – or in this case don't want it – to do.'

I certainly hoped that was true, because last time I'd

been around Fee at full moon she'd wolfed out, despite insisting she had it under control.

I was distracted from my worries by the chatter all around. The flowers were watching our every move, and commenting loudly. Their voices sounded ever so gossipy.

'Look, they're coming now,' said a tiger-lily.

'Isn't that one cute?' said a daisy.

'What, the floppy-haired boy or the one with the fetching monocle?' asked a rose.

'Oh, I'd fetch his monocle,' said the daisy. 'I'd fetch anything he asked me to.'

Oh dear. Hugo had a strange sort of attraction as far as some women – and statues, and werewolves, and now talking flowers, it seemed – were concerned. As far as *I* was concerned, Jake was definitely the cute one.

'Come closer,' said the daisy. 'Come here and talk to me, Alice, and tell me if your friend is single.'

'I'm Annie,' I corrected, my voice a slow, dull drawl. This air was really beginning to get to me. It was as though it was invading my mind. I felt sleepy and stupid, and all I wanted was my own bed.

'Oh.' The daisy looked at me sceptically. 'Are you sure about that? I thought you were Alice, because you look nothing like her.'

'That makes no sense,' Fee told the flower with a growl. She tried to say more, but her voice was not in her favour. All that came out was some guttural snarling. Yikes. Her eyes were completely yellow now, and her nails were looking awfully sharp.

'Come closer, Annie-not-Alice,' said the daisy

(somehow acting as though Fee *wasn't* incredibly terrifying). 'And I'll tell you how to get to the tea party. That's where you want to get to, isn't it?'

I hesitated. Could this flower really be Ralph's contact? If so, I wished he could have chosen something much less creepy. There was a whole face on the seedhead at the centre of her petals, including slits for eyes and a sharp-toothed mouth. Those were blooming vampire teeth (pun unintended). As if a flower with facial features wasn't weird enough, this one had to go and be a *vampire* plant, too? It was growing larger and larger before my eyes. Right now, with Fee close to turning, a giant, bloodthirsty daisy was the last thing I needed.

And yet, I was leaning, closer and closer, as though I couldn't stop myself…

'I wouldn't get too close, if I were you,' said a languid voice from somewhere to the south. I jumped back from the vampire daisy and turned at the sound. A few feet away from us, where the garden bordered a pond, a caterpillar was lounging atop an enormous mushroom, smoking a hookah. At the sight of him, a swell of shock surged through me.

The caterpillar wasn't supposed to be in this part of the prison world, was he? Plus, the one Alice met in the first book was only three inches high, but this caterpillar was just as big as any of us. Perhaps this version of Wonderland was even wonkier than Laine knew.

Fee growled, but somehow managed to gain enough control to say, 'That caterpillar is smoking a bloody *hookah*. That's why we could smell smoke in Ralph's office. But … I'm kind of freaked out that we could smell it through the mirror, back before we ever got swallowed by it.'

'He must be our contact,' guessed Hugo.

'That I am,' the caterpillar confirmed as we approached. 'Those flowers have no intention of letting you anywhere near that tea party. They've been got to.'

While I puzzled at his words – and at his being where he shouldn't be – Jake gave me a gentle nudge. 'Annie, the trees are moving,' he said, pointing to the forest. 'It's like … like something really big is moving through.'

With a gulp, I saw that he was right. Something enormous was moving towards us, coming through the trees and moving fast. As if we didn't have enough to deal with.

'Oh, that's a Bandersnatch coming,' said the caterpillar. 'You don't want to get caught by one of them, I can tell you, or you'll meet your end. I can help you get away in time, but I need to be certain you've not been rendered completely dumb. It's the air, you know – it's designed to repel Bandersnatches, but newcomers can find themselves getting a little confused, too. Tell me, woman with auburn hair, can you recite the Abstinence Song?'

'Of course,' said Fee, suddenly perking up at the mention of her favourite ditty. 'I'd know it in my sleep. It goes:

"*Nothing's as good for angels as acceptance,*

Acceptance, acceptance, it's always the way to act…"'

She shook her head with frustration. 'No, that's not right. It's … what is it? What are the right words?'

'It's already too late, then,' the caterpillar told her.

'For you, at least, werewolf. Not only is the enchanted air already having an effect on you, but the moon is too. You're turning.'

'But I'm–' Fee had most likely been about to insist she was reformed, but once again, her words descended into some sort of guttural snarl.

'Well then,' said the caterpillar. 'I shall just leave you to it.' He took a deep puff and turned his gaze on me. 'Annie, can you remember the poem I was going to ask *you* to recite?'

Despite his riddle-talk, I thought I knew what he meant. 'The poem Alice recites to the caterpillar in the book?' I guessed.

'Indeed.'

'Well, it's ...' I scratched my head, feeling frustrated. I couldn't even bring the name of the poem to mind, let alone the words. All of my preparation was no match for the enchanted air. I looked desperately at Jake. 'Can you remember it?'

Jake met my eyes, terror in his. 'I know I *did* remember it, but all of a sudden it's like the words are all backwards in my mind. If I could just write them down ...'

'There's no time for that,' stated the caterpillar, pointing his hookah at the forest. 'That Bandersnatch is getting closer. Oh, but luckily, here comes someone to help you.' He pointed to a man who suddenly rushed past, trying his best not to look our way. Well ... not *exactly* a man. As I peered closer I saw that he was one of those twitchy White Rabbit Guards, dressed in his blue and white uniform, just like the ones at the Museum of Never Again.

'He won't be the cat's pyjamas,' the caterpillar continued after taking another puff of his pipe. 'But he might give you a whisker of a chance.'

My mind cleared slightly at his words. 'Whisker, that's it! That's how the rogue guards escaped the museum. They made a portal in the ground when one of them chucked down a hair from his moustache! But ...' I gazed after the running guard. 'He seems like he's running really hard, but ... he's not moving very far at all.'

The caterpillar smiled lazily. 'Round these parts, you need to run twice as fast to get anywhere. When he makes a hole, follow him down it. Hopefully you'll get into the right side of Wonkyland, and start to think more clearly, before your friend turns.'

I glanced at Fee. Her eyes were deep yellow, as she sounded a low, steady growl.

'It's happening, Annie,' she told me. 'And I don't think I can stop it.'

'You can't,' said the caterpillar. He then nodded down to the mushroom he sat upon. 'Take as much as you can and stick it in your pockets. Remember – one side makes you bigger, and the other side makes you littler. Always good to be prepared.'

Panicking, I reached out to the mushroom and pulled off some pieces. Jake and Hugo took some too. They had the good sense to ask the caterpillar which side did what, but he didn't reply; he simply slithered down off the mushroom and moved away, smoking contentedly as he went, not looking back at us at all.

Once we'd filled our pockets, we looked nervously at Fee. She was crouching now, her limbs elongating, her nose growing longer, her hands and arms beginning to sprout hairs. If the air wasn't making us feel so dull, we probably would have done something about it – what, I don't know, but something.

'Run!' she roared. 'Before I do something I might regret.'

With a sorrowful stare at Fee, Jake grabbed my hand. 'We've got to go, Annie – the rabbity man might not be moving fast, but he *is* moving. Hugo – you too. We will get Fee back, I promise you. But right now, we've got to go.'

Hugo nodded, tears forming in the corners of his eyes, and the three of us took off at a run.

As we chased the White Rabbit Guard, Fee howled at the moon, and then began to chase after us. I could see that she was doing her best *not* to chase us – she would sometimes stop short, shaking her head and even turning around, but always starting after us again, despite her best efforts. And there was hunger in her eyes – such incredible hunger. If she did catch us, we wouldn't last long. In her current state, we probably looked as good to her as steak tartare.

While we pursued the rabbit and Fee pursued us, I saw something else behind my friend, in the distance, but closing in on us much faster than *we* were closing in on the guard. It had long, long legs. I couldn't make out much more about it, because the rest of it was so tall. But I had the terrifying certainty that if I craned my neck, I'd know *exactly* what frumious jaws looked like.

I ran so hard my chest burned. At points during that run I felt like we weren't getting anywhere, but we pushed and pushed until finally we were only a foot away from the guard. He yanked out one of his whiskers, chucked it at the ground, and an almighty hole appeared.

'Here goes everything!' Jake cried, as the three of us jumped into nothingness.

CHAPTER 9
WE'RE ALL MAD HERE

It really did feel like we were surrounded by nothing, to begin with, as we fell downwards at a dizzying speed. After a while, I began to see what looked like the rounded walls of a well. A little after that, I saw shelving, and paintings and maps on pegs, and a tempting jar of marmalade. And then ... then we landed on an enormous pile of leaves.

I still felt dreamy, my thoughts backwards and bonkers, but ever so slightly *less* backwards and bonkers than they'd been in the garden. I didn't sit up immediately, because I had managed to land on top of Jake, and the sensation of him below me was far too nice to bring to an end.

'Come on, guys,' said Hugo, shaking my arm and bringing me back to reality. 'We've got to figure out a plan for Fee.'

Jake gave me a look of regret as I dragged myself off him and stood up – or tried to stand up, anyway. We'd landed in a long, low hall, and I had to hunch to stop my head from banging against the ceiling. Ahead of us, the hallway was lined with closed doors.

'You're right, Hugo,' I agreed. 'Figuring out what to do with Fee has got to take first place. Because even if we get the teapot, we'll need her back in her normal state – I mean, unless we fancy wrestling a werewolf into submission and shoving her through the mirror so we can all get home.' I let out a groan of frustration. 'This isn't gonna be easy, is it?'

Jake squeezed my hand. 'Not easy, maybe. But absolutely doable. I don't know about you guys, but my head has really cleared. I can recall the books pretty clearly, so getting to the tea party should be easy enough. And as for Fee, well … what we need is some sort of No-Turn potion. Most of them are made with yellow wolfsbane as the main ingredient, and I know what that looks like and how to mix up a simple emergency shot, so we can keep our eyes out for what we need along the way.'

I shook my head in wonder. 'How do you know how to make a No-Turn potion?'

Jake sighed. 'A story for another day. First, we need to get out of this hall – and according to Alice's Adventures in Wonderland, there should be a key on a three-legged table – a key that'll unlock a super-tiny door. Of course, we'll need to shrink ourselves before we can get through said door, but I'm sure we can manage that. We've already got the mushroom pieces, and we'll find other foodstuffs near the table that can make us bigger or littler, too.'

Hugo clapped him on the back. 'I'm impressed, Jake.

And there I was, positive that without Laine we'd be totally lost.'

With that half-compliment, half-insult, he took off at a brisk walk (sometimes a brisk crawl, when the tunnel got too low), and Jake and I followed him. It didn't take us long to find the table, and just as in the book, we also found a bottle labelled 'Drink Me' and a small cake labelled 'Eat Me'.

With the three of us, things went far more quickly than they had for Alice. Sure, it took us a few experiments to figure out which potions, cakes and mushroom pieces would make us bigger or smaller, but Hugo volunteered to be our guinea pig. ('Anything for Fee and Dora,' he'd proudly declared, which would have been lovely had he not added: 'And for the teapot, of course – mustn't forget the teapot.') If we overshot things a little we were soon able to get him back to the right height, and before we knew it we were out in Wonderland, avoiding many of the pitfalls and confusing interactions Alice had met along her way.

It all felt a little too easy, which bothered me. At points I felt like I wasn't only working with my knowledge of the books. It felt as if I was remembering things, as if I *knew* this place, and had been through it all before. The dream I'd been having this week was niggling at me again. It couldn't have been real though, could it? Me, here with Hugo when we were children, facing off against a crimson-haired queen?

I thought about saying something to Hugo – especially when, once or twice, he suddenly paused to frown at something as though *he* was finding it all a bit familiar, too. But every time I attempted to broach it, it was as though the words were suddenly lost to me. I'd find myself daydreaming about something entirely different, and by the time I snapped my mind back to the subject, Hugo would be rushing onwards once more.

However frustrating it might be, I knew that he was right to rush. We really didn't have time for long discussions about my crazy dreams, or my lost wand, or any of it. Not if we were going to get out of here – and rescue Fee and Dora, too. But if I could talk to him just for a minute, about ... wait, what *was* it that I needed to tell him again?

I let out a gasp as I saw a clearing ahead of us. In that clearing there was a house with a fur-thatched roof and unusually-shaped chimneys – the chimneys were elongated, almost like the ears of a rabbit or a hare.

'Well, that has to be the March Hare's house,' Jake said, spying it at the same time. 'We're here.'

Jake and I quickened our footsteps, but Hugo stopped short. There was something on the path, right in front of him: a cat.

The cat didn't appear all at once. First I saw the grin – and it was a sharp-fanged grin, looking every bit as vampiric as the flowers we'd met. Next I saw the eyes and ears, then the rest of it.

This must be the Cheshire Cat. His slow appearance was a little like those moments when Jake faded back in again after being invisible. Only ... I glanced at Jake ... he *still* hadn't faded out, not even once since this whole misadventure began. I wasn't about to tell him I was proud of him (how patronising would *that* be?) but I really was glad to have him by my side.

For a moment Hugo's face lit up, and he bent down and patted the cat. As the cat purred, Hugo turned to me as if he was about to say something, but a shadow entered his eyes, and instead of speaking he shook his head and straightened up, stepping to the left of the cat.

The cat mirrored him, blocking his path again. They went on that way for a few seconds more until Hugo lost his cool and said, 'Look, kitty cat, if you don't politely step aside, I'm going to have to manhandle you.'

With a haughty expression, the cat said, 'Oh, are you now? And I thought you were a cat lover.'

'I *am*,' Hugo said. 'But I'm also in a hurry, so can you please just move out of my way. We have places to be.'

'Oh, I know exactly where you're going,' said the Cheshire Cat. 'And I think it's a much better idea if you all come along with me instead. There's a friend of mine approaching through the woods just now, and I think you ought to meet him.'

As the cat spoke in a lazy drawl, the forest began to move, as it had once before. The trees were being knocked over as though they were mere twigs, and the size and speed of whatever was moving through them was large enough to create a strong breeze.

'Annie,' said Jake, a note of warning in his voice. 'I think it's the Bandersnatch. How could it catch us up so fast? Is it even supposed to be in this part of the realm?'

'No,' I replied, unable to hide my worry. The caterpillar, the Bandersnatch ... so much was in the wrong place. And so much of it had stupid vampire teeth, too. Ciara certainly liked to mix things up, which did not bode well for us. What if we got to the tea party, and there was no teapot? 'I'm getting the impression that there's more than one Bandersnatch in this place. Something *else* I wasn't warned about – thank you Laine and Ralph. We'd better get going.'

'Oh, don't be hasty,' said the cat. 'You're much better off with a Bandersnatch than with the Queen – or worse, with my mistress, the Duchess. Come on, now. Come with me.'

Hugo rolled his eyes, picked the cat up, and set it to the side of the path. 'You're not going to fool *us,* buddy. If a Bandersnatch is coming, we're certainly not going to go running towards its frumious jaws.'

As we tried to walk on, the cat leapt into Hugo's face, crying, 'No! I can't let you go that way. You have to come with me.'

'Are you *mad* cat?' Hugo cried, clawing the cat off his face. He showed great patience, not flinging it away from him but laying it gently aside.

'We're all mad here,' the cat announced with a sigh, looking plaintively at Hugo but refraining from a second attack. 'It's because of Ciara. She always manages to get into our heads, no matter how hard we work to keep her out. But I can teach you how to control it. I–' The cat cut himself off, his eyes widening as he looked to his left.

A dozen rabbity men were streaking towards us, with murder in their eyes.

'Remember!' the cat said, his voice remaining long after his body had disappeared. 'Remember how you got out of here before!'

CHAPTER 10
PIGS SHALL FLY

For a moment we ran, but it soon became clear that the White Rabbit Guards had no interest in us. The men turned in the other direction, crying out, 'Here, puss-puss! We've got some nice treats for you. Won't you come out and say hello?'

So, with the Cheshire Cat's words ringing in my ears, we slowed our steps once more, and headed to the March Hare's garden.

I turned to Hugo, about to say something about the cat, but the words fizzled out at the tip of my tongue, and all I could focus on was the scene before me.

A long table, situated in the shade of a tree, was laid out for tea. Unlike in the book, there were four at the party instead of three.

The first was the Hatter, who looked like I'd imagined: he wore a large top hat which sat askew, and a suit that had seen better days. The second, the March Hare, was also as I'd imagined – basically, a giant hare who walked upright. He wore a rather fetching velvet waistcoat and some corduroy slacks.

And then there was Dora, who I'd been longing to see. The Hare and the Hatter were pulling her from her cup, trying to cram her into the teapot. They seemed to think it was great fun altogether, saying, 'Tell us the story, Dora – you know the one we want!' while she yawned and complained.

The fourth at the party, the one I *didn't* expect, was a woman who stood a few feet from the table: a tall woman with crimson-red hair and a ruby crown upon her head. I knew, without a doubt, that this was Ciara, the Queen of Minds. The woman from my dreams. She looked directly at me and smiled, revealing sharp, dangerous fangs.

The March Hare hopped excitedly up and down and said, 'She's here, she's here – are we going to change places?' As he spoke, he hopped to the next seat along, taking Dora and the teapot with him.

'No, no, no,' said the Queen, stomping to the table, yanking Dora from the teapot and shoving her back in a cup – the very cup she'd been in every time she came to visit me. 'Not yet – they've only just gotten here. First, I want to take Annie to play croquet and have her do one or two errands for me. *Then* we'll have our tea party.'

Dora spun her head and, in her lovely, sleepy voice, said, 'Annie is here?' Her little eyes met my gaze and she added, 'Oh no, oh no, oh no. You shouldn't have come, my witch. This is exactly what she wanted!'

'Shush up now!' bellowed Queen Ciara. 'Or I'll be

into your head, Dora, and you don't like it when I do that, do you?'

Dora quivered, and as I rushed forward to grab her, the ground shook beneath my feet, and my eyes grew drowsy.

∼

IT WOULDN'T BE RIGHT TO SAY THAT I CAME BACK TO MY SENSES – my senses, if anything, felt fuzzier than ever – but I certainly regained consciousness. I had no idea how much time had passed when I woke up, no longer in the March Hare's garden, but in an altogether different place. Jake, Hugo and I had been transported somehow, along with the Queen of Minds. Dora, as well as the Hatter and the Hare, had been left behind.

We stood on uneven ground, with a croquet game in progress all around us. The area was surrounded with white rose bushes. A group of terrified-looking gardeners were hurriedly painting the flowers red.

None of the people had playing cards for bodies, the way they had in *Alice*. Instead, they all wore lavish costumes with cards emblazoned on lapels, or worked into the design. Thankfully, the balls seemed to have hedgehog faces painted on, rather than being actual hedgehogs, and the mallets were painted flamingo-pink instead of being live flamingos.

Ciara shoved some mallets into our hands, and said, 'Let's talk while we play.'

As Jake, Hugo and I followed her, three others played close to us, watching our every move. One of the three made me feel super uneasy. She was a short, curvy woman who smelled strongly of pepper. She wore a dark dress and a darker smile. The other two were men: a handsome vampire with a Knave of Hearts playing card stitched onto his lapel, and a quivering, frightened-looking member of the White Rabbit Guard.

The curvy woman seemed very keen on Hugo, her eyes greedily following him. There was something so familiar about the way she looked at him, and it kept coming to the forefront of my mind, only to be whisked away again before I could fully recall.

My mental turmoil made a confusing game all the more baffling. The hoops, through which we should have been hitting the balls, were constantly on the move. It wouldn't have mattered if they *had* stayed still, because the hedgehog balls didn't move in straight lines anyway. The Queen was somehow winning (according to her) despite playing just as uselessly as the rest of us.

Every now and then I thought I spied the enormous grin of the Cheshire Cat, peeping out at us from a bush or a hedge, but he always disappeared before I could be sure he was there.

I went along with the madness, waiting for one of two things to happen: either my mind would un-muddy itself and come up with a wonderful plan, or the Queen of Minds would tell us what she wanted.

'I think it's time I told you what I want,' she said.

I sighed. 'Yeah, that sounds about right.'

'But first, introductions. That's my closest friend, the talented witch known as the Duchess,' said Ciara, nodding to the curvy woman. 'We built this world together, the Duchess and I. The good-looking man is my beau, the Knave. He's an incorrigible thief, but I forgive him for that, because he's stolen my heart.' She laughed uproariously at her corny joke, before dragging him in for a sloppy kiss.

When she'd embarrassed us all quite enough, she broke away and said, 'And that pathetic rabbity looking fellow standing near us is Mr White, a senior member of the White Rabbit Guard.' She tossed a smug look at Mr White. 'Give it long enough, and *everyone* becomes my loyal follower, whether they want to or not. In fact, many members of the White Rabbit Guard have betrayed their horrible faery queen and have come over to my side instead.'

'Gee, you don't say,' Jake drawled.

The Queen looked at him with interest. 'You're enormously good-looking, which is nice and everything, but I don't know who you *are*. I know who Hugo is, of course, although his presence is just as much of a surprise as yours. Annie was supposed to come with the treasure hunter, not with you two.'

'Supposed to?' said Hugo. 'So this was all planned? Does my father ... no, he wouldn't work for *you*. Would he?'

I dreaded the answer as much as Hugo did. It was bad enough being under Ralph's thumb, but if his thumb happened to be a truly evil one...

'Hah!' She snorted, as though the very idea was absurd. 'I'm sorry-not-sorry to have to tell you this, Hugo, but I was a step ahead of your father the whole time. Ralph believed Mr White here to be his informant, you see. Mr White let it "slip" that a teapot Ralph wanted very badly would be back in my realm and ripe for the picking very soon, after being stolen from the fae queen's museum by some of Mr White's colleagues. He led Ralph to believe that the job would be easy enough. He gave him routes to follow, mentioning places at which contacts would be waiting to help things along. He told him how to avoid my notice, and even dropped some hints that certain aspects of the job would be especially suited to Annie. Though why, after all of these years as a collector, Ralph actually believed that stealing something of mine could be so easy, I'll never know.'

So it *was* a trap. Wonderful. Well, at least Ralph wasn't quite as evil as I'd feared. Reckless, maybe. Dishonest, definitely. But not evil. I glanced at Hugo to see if the news had cheered him up, but he didn't seem remotely happy. He was looking at me, then at the Queen, then at me again.

'Is that recognition I see in your eyes, Hugo?' said Queen Ciara. 'Oh, the Duchess *will* be happy about that.' She glanced at her friend. 'Won't you, my dear?'

'Very,' agreed the Duchess with a smirk.

Hugo's eyes widened. 'I'm not going mad, am I? This all happened before!' He grasped my arm and said, 'It did, Annie. That horrible witch tried to turn me into ... into *something*. But then ... what happened then?' His eyes brightened with excitement, and he tugged at my sleeve. 'Oh, I remember now. The Queen of Minds, she wants you–'

Whatever he was about to say was cut off, as the Duchess outstretched a finger and rendered him immobile. 'That's quite enough of that,' she said. Still pointing her finger, she mumbled some words. Hugo shrank and transformed in front of us, squealing as he was turned into a small pig. I'd never seen a pig wear a tweed suit, a waistcoat, a dickey bow and a monocle before, but there was a first time for everything.

'Not *quite* right,' the Duchess murmured. 'Ah, yes, I wanted to make him fly the last time he was here, didn't I?' With some more mumbled words, tiny holes appeared in the back of his outfit, through which little pink wings began to push out. Hugo seemed to have no control over those wings; as they began to flap, he rose reluctantly into the sky, squealing out in terror.

'What the heck did you do that for?!' I cried, throwing my mallet to the ground.

'And *how* the heck did you do it?' Jake shouted, chucking his own mallet across the grass, where it landed in a pond. 'How come you can use magic when we can't? You're a *prisoner*.'

The Duchess and Ciara shared a smirk, before Ciara answered for her friend, saying, 'That's certainly true. But long before this was a prison it was a world controlled by my mind. Inside here, everything that happens is *still* controlled by my mind – including who gets to have magic and who doesn't. The Duchess is on my side, so she gets to keep her power. You three on the other hand ... well, you're hardly friends of mine, are you?'

'Just tell me what you want with me,' I snarled. 'You wanted me in here for some reason, right? If I do whatever it is you want me to do, will you turn Hugo back? Fee back?'

Ciara gave me a calculating gaze. 'You cut to the chase, don't you, Annie? I rather like that.'

'I don't give a crap what you like,' I told her.

'But you *do* give a crap about Dora?' She smiled slyly. 'Oh yes, you do – even after all of these years. Hugo seemed to remember – or at least he was beginning to. But you ... I rather think Ralph used a much stronger memory spell on you, Annie. Because *I* certainly wouldn't want you to forget your first time here. Seven-year-old you was far superior to whatever it is you've become as an adult. Hugo was a lot more interesting when he was younger, too. Back then, he was a man – or a boy, I suppose – of action. These days, I hear he's nothing but a toady for his dad.'

'Look, vampire,' said Jake, balling his fists. 'Talking in circles and making sly little digs isn't going to get you very far, is it? So maybe get to the point.'

She ignored him and focused on me. 'You must be wondering how you got in here all those years ago? Back when you were seven, and your father took you to the museum. It seemed he found you very boring company. So much so that he downed a bottle of wine and fell asleep in a throne once owned by some evil stepmother or other. You left him to it, and went off exploring with Hugo. Children make friends so easily, don't they?' She took a pause, a misty-eyed expression on her face.

'In a dusty storeroom,' she went on, 'you and Hugo found an old, old mirror which Ralph had purchased from one of his less salubrious sellers. Ralph didn't know it at the time, but that mirror was a long-closed portal to my world. You looked into that mirror, and Dora – who is *always* wandering off – was looking right back at you. The moment she saw you, she decided that you were her witch and she your familiar. It was rather a slap in the face for me, mind you. Because you see, Dora was supposed to be *my* familiar.'

'You're a vampire, not a witch,' I pointed out.

'Well, some vampires have familiars. Haven't you ever heard of Renfield?'

'That's a whole different thing,' Jake argued. 'Forcing someone to be in your thrall is nothing like a witch having a natural bond with a magical animal.'

'Well I don't *need* a natural bond,' she scoffed. 'Not when I have the Duchess to create a bonding spell for me. I'd always wanted a dormouse, ever since I read *Alice*, you see – and my friend's spell was strong. So strong that, when the innocents were being rescued all those years ago, poor Dora had no choice but to say that she'd willingly worked alongside me.'

She let out a harsh, horrible laugh. 'The faery queen didn't believe her. She took a shine to Dora – even let her keep her favourite cup. But Dora kept on insisting she had helped me in all of my plans, because she *couldn't* say otherwise. It was hilarious, really it was. Because that stupid little mouse was never on my side. Oh, I tried to make her behave more like the rest of us, but she was always lecturing me about right and wrong. I was almost relieved when you arrived to take her off my hands.'

I stared at her in frustration, wishing I could remember *any* of this. 'But you still haven't explained how I *got* here,' I hissed. 'How on earth did I get through that mirror if all portals to this world had been shut to anyone but the White Rabbit Guard?'

'It was a big surprise to us all, really it was. The Duchess believes it happened because of your bond with Dora. It is a true bond, and a strong one, so she tells me. The sort that can break through barriers. But I wasn't about to let you just take her. I had the Duchess strengthen my own bonding spell with Dora – enough to make sure she couldn't leave with you, not unless I said so. And then, I set you a little task. You were to win at chess, so that you could become a queen. Become my equal. Then, and only then, would I allow you to take Dora home.

'I wasn't really all that surprised when you failed,' she continued. 'I suppose Dora just didn't matter enough to you, or you'd have put more effort in. So you went home with your tail between your legs. Ralph must have spied you and Hugo coming back through, and messed with your memories. Recently, I've allowed Dora to go through from time to time – your bond made it possible for her to do that, even if you didn't remember her. She was convinced you'd come for her again some day – that you'd remember her, and return to the museum to seek her out. And then one day you *did* return, but not for Dora.'

She placed a hand on her chest and sighed dramatically. 'Oh, her poor little heart was broken, Annie. Absolutely broken. If you'd fully believed her when she told you she was your familiar, you see, she would have been able to stay put in your world as long as she liked. It would have completely undone the Duchess's false-bonding spell, and set Dora free. But ... you never accepted her.'

She boffed me over the head with her mallet. 'And so my poor little Dora had to come back to me, each and every time. And you're stuck here now because your heart is *still* filled with suspicion. It's your *bond* that's the key, remember – so if you'd fully embraced it, that portal would never have closed behind you today. But you had to go and let the doubts creep into your heart, because that's just how you *are,* isn't it? I predicted as much, long before you arrived this time around. My plan to trap you here hinged on the fact that I *knew* you had no faith in your bond. Why on earth Dora loves you so much is a mystery to me.'

Rubbing my head, I glared at her, feeling miserable. Dora had told me, very recently, that it was important I believed she was my familiar. I'd thought I *did* believe, but clearly I didn't have enough faith.

And the fact that it was our bond which opened the portal, well that explained all of the questions Laine kept asking me. Every time I was at that mirror, he'd grilled me about her. He knew that there was never any portal key. There was only me, and my strange connection with the dormouse. It must have been one of those things Mr White had let 'slip' to Ralph.

But all of that aside, there were parts of her story which made no sense.

Hands on my hips, I said, 'So you just let me, a seven-year-old girl, go? The first one to come here in over a hundred years? I don't believe you.'

'Sceptical then, sceptical now. That much hasn't changed. Well, I *did* let you go, actually. There's a route which anyone who's not a prisoner here can use to escape, but ... maybe I'll keep the details to myself this time around.'

'It doesn't matter if you tell us how we can get out of here or not, you evil freak,' Jake spat. 'We can figure it out for ourselves. And if we don't, people will miss us. They'll come for us. And when they do, I'm betting the conditions in this prison will get a whole lot worse for you.'

She whacked a ball directly at the head of one of the gardeners and said, 'Oh, I'm sure you're right. But what with teatime lasting ever so long in my world, it could be ages before your rescuers arrive. And so much can happen in that time. Little accidents, you know. Werewolves getting torn apart by Bandersnatches. Monocled men getting stuck in pig form by a spell so strong that, even when you *do* get rescued, it could take years to break it. And if that's not bad enough, I hear that pots of tea are awfully dangerous this time of year. An ungrateful little dormouse could positively drown in one...'

Jake's jaw grew steel-hard, and his eyes glinted with rage. For a moment I thought he might pick up another mallet and start hitting people, but he calmed himself down and said, 'You're threatening us, obviously, but what you still haven't told us is *why*. Why did you do all of this? Lure Annie here? Make your minions commit theft and murder at the Museum of Never Again? What is it that you want?'

She gave him a toothy smile. 'Why, to reunite Annie

and Dora, of course. And I'm feeling rather impatient today, so there'll be no time for chatting with Mock Turtles or figuring out who stole the tarts. Instead I'm going to have my friend, the Gryphon, take you straight to the chess board. He spells his title differently than your museum's Griffin does, so mind how you address him.'

'How will he know how we're *spelling* his name?' Jake questioned. Then with a sigh, he said, 'Never mind. What happens at the chess board?'

'Annie will play as a White Pawn. Jake, you shall help her. The two of you shall be taken to the edge of the second square, and a train will take you across the third – but it won't be as easy as I'm making it sound. You'll have to answer a series of questions to advance, proving to me your knowledge of my world. If Annie wins and becomes a queen, *then* I'll allow you all out of here alive. You have my guarantee that your friends will turn back into their usual forms, and you can even have both Dora *and* the teapot.'

'That all sounds too good to be true,' said Jake.

She gave us a saccharine smile. 'I swear to you, I tell you no lies.'

'Hm.' I eyed her warily. Whenever someone insisted they weren't lying, I automatically became convinced that they were. It came from my father, I think. He would so often swear he hadn't been the one to drink all of Granny's wine, or to have thrown anything flavourful into the bin. And then there was Chickpea, Dad's familiar, who had sworn yet again only this morning that he was vegetarian, while chowing down on cold roast beef.

Ciara was a bigger liar than both of them combined, I just *sensed* it. If only Hugo hadn't been changed, maybe he would have told an entirely different story to the one I'd just heard. But he was a pig now. I glanced worriedly up at the sky. I couldn't even see him anymore. He must be terrified.

Ciara tapped a foot impatiently. 'Decided to say yes, yet?'

'We've decided we don't trust you,' said Jake. 'And our decision was made in an instant. Maybe it's because you've just got one of those faces. Or maybe, I dunno, it's because you're an evil vampire who's been imprisoned for kidnapping little girls.'

'Oh, look, I can't do anything about your sad, sad cynicism,' she retorted. 'You can refuse, of course, and try to find your own way to fix the problem. You can even do nothing, and pray that the treasure hunter comes to save you. Though as I believe I've made clear, certain accidents *will* happen in the meantime. But look ... here comes your ride, so it's make up your mind time.'

A huge griffin (sorry, gryphon) began to fly onto the croquet ground. It was kind of weird to see one that *wasn't* a statue, but instead had real live wings and talons and a great big golden beak.

As Ciara waved him down, she said, 'Better get on board. And once he drops you off, remember – be on your guard for Red Knights and Bandersnatches...'

CHAPTER 11
PLAYING THE GAME

The flight was a letdown. Back in the real world, I'd had the odd fantasy of the museum's Griffin coming to life and saying, 'Get on board, Annie.' In those daydreams, our flights together had been exhilarating. But this Wonky Wonderland creature, though made of feathers, fur and flesh, was far stonier than the Griffin back home.

He said absolutely nothing to us for ages, not until we got back to the *Looking Glass* portion of the world. Then, after swooping down onto what appeared to be the second square in the chessboard-patterned countryside, he suddenly decided to speak, saying, 'Get off, will you? And be quick about it.'

As we scrambled onto the ground, he added, 'Tell your Griff I said, "What's up?"' before soaring off into the sky.

'He wasn't much like the Gryphon in *Alice*, was he?' remarked Jake as he stretched out his limbs (the flight had *not* been a comfortable one). 'But you know what's funny? I almost think that if we did tell our museum Griffin that that guy said, "What's up?" he'd probably understand. Our statue feels ... I dunno. Like, every time I'm sitting at Hugo's desk I'm waiting for him to suddenly start speaking, y'know?'

'Yeah, he's pretty lifelike,' I agreed, because after a day like the one we'd been having, stubborn denial felt senseless. Of course, when Laine had said something similar I'd been evasive because, well, he was Laine. I might share a gift and a secret with the treasure hunter, but things felt easier, safer, with Jake. I almost wished they could swap places – except that I wouldn't wish Laine's situation, or my own, on anyone.

We gazed around, getting our bearings. When we'd been looking down upon it during the flight, the pattern in the ground had been so obvious. But now that we were down here, each square was so big that it was impossible to tell we were even in one.

We found some yellow wolfsbane pretty quickly (I would have to take Jake's word on it, as my knowledge of plant life was far from spectacular). He gathered more things as we moved along – pieces of wood, stone, other flowers and herbs. I wasn't sure what he was up to at first, but it soon began to make sense.

Somehow, with a combination of what he'd found and what he had in his pockets, he'd fashioned a makeshift bow and some arrows, and even made a quiver to store the arrows. He'd also emptied out a small paint tin and used it to mix up the No-Turn potion, before smearing it on the arrowheads.

'So when you talked about an emergency *shot* for Fee, you really meant it,' I observed.

'I really did. But I've had a lot of practice at this, and I know just where to hit her so it won't hurt a bit. She'll be knocked out for the briefest moment, and then she'll turn back into Fee. And if we're lucky – depending on what she's eaten as a wolf – she might not even be hangry anymore.'

I let out a laugh. I was learning so much about Jake today. That he was funny, brave, and resourceful, and that he knew how to give evil vampire queens about as much backtalk as they deserved. Each new thing made me like him even more.

'I can't believe all of the stuff you have in your pockets,' I said. 'Knives, string, a tiny hammer and chisel, paint tins and glues, filing tools, and so many things I can't even identify...'

'Yeah, well I like to be prepared. I put *bigger on the inside* spells on my pockets so I can fill 'em up.'

As we walked along, chattering and preparing more arrows, it began to grow hotter. Insects buzzed around us, the air thick with them.

Jake laughed with delight as he spied them. 'They're proper *Alice* insects – rocking-horse-flies and bread-and-butter-flies. Can you believe it? Their heads are really made from lumps of sugar!'

While we were gazing in fascination at the crazy-looking insects all around us, they suddenly swooped, opening their mouths and revealing that – like so many things in this place – they had sharp, greedy fangs. And the insects were keen to use those fangs, dashing at our skin and biting us all over.

But because Jake was full of surprises today, he was able to whip up a balm which calmed down the soreness, and kept the insects away. It smelled eye-wateringly strong, but it definitely worked.

'I think I prefer the insects back home,' he commented, once he'd smeared some balm on his last bite. 'We jump the brook now, right?' He pointed at a fast-flowing stream ahead of us and, beyond that, what appeared to be a train platform. 'Only...'

'The brook looks wider than you thought it'd be?' I sighed. 'Yeah, me too. If we fall in, I guess we could swim. But the current looks scarily strong.'

'It does. But over there looks *way* better than this bloody square – see how there's none of those vicious insects on the other side. Of course, it could be a mirage, and when we get over there there'll be twice as many.'

'Oh, you optimist, you. I guess ... I guess we just have to go for it, yeah?'

It wasn't the most enticing prospect, but Jake somehow managed to give me a bright smile. 'Yeah, sounds about right,' he said. 'Hold hands for luck?'

I let him grasp his hand in mine, hoping mine wasn't too clammy (as always, I was laser-focused on the task). We took the brook at a running jump, feeling that same sensation as we had when we travelled down the stairs – it was like we were floating in a dreamlike way, and the journey over the brook was far easier than we'd expected. When we got to the other side, a steam train was puffing to a stop at the platform, and every waiting passenger was an animal.

'Tickets, please!' a guard bellowed, rushing towards us and peering at us through opera glasses.

'Oh yeah ... tickets ...' I patted my pockets, hoping that they'd somehow magically appear, but there was nothing inside other than some lip balm and my coin purse. 'If you could just direct us to the ticket office.'

'You gots the right currency?'

'We gots ...' Good grief, his strange accent was catching. 'I mean, we've got money.' I fished out some of the usual coins from back home: stars, sickles and rounds. 'Will any of these do?'

'No, no, no – we trade in questions here, missy – ain't you been told? You gots to answer the questions, you does. You – dark-haired lady – how much you think them puffs of smoke coming out the train is worth?'

'Oh!' I found myself bouncing excitedly on my heels. 'Oh, I know this. This is from the book.'

'Answer, lady!'

'Okay, okay,' I said. 'It's worth a thousand pounds a puff.'

'Good, you can go on, dark-haired lady. And you, brown-eyed boy, what's a bread-and-butter-fly live on?'

Jake, with a grin of knowing, replied: 'Weak tea and cream.'

∽

As we sat on board the train, huddled close together, I think we both knew what was at stake here – we had to play Ciara's game, at least until we knew of some other way of getting Dora, and getting out of here with Hugo and Fee in their preferred physical forms. It was terrifying, it really was ... and yet ... I felt such a buzz, just sitting close to Jake, crammed in amongst all the strange creatures – a goat, a beetle, a horse, and even a hoarse-sounding gnat.

There was so much going on around us, and yet none of it seemed to matter. Sitting beside Jake, hand in hand, with him being so utterly positive and brave throughout the whole mess ... it made it all seem surmountable. Like when a nightmare suddenly becomes lucid, and you just *know* you'll slay the monster and kiss the prince – you can control it all, and give it the ending you want, as though it's a story you're writing in your sleep.

As he pointed to yet another wonder out the window (a great marble statue of a sleeping Queen Ciara), I glanced at him, my heart beating fast, thinking: sometime soon we were going to get together, and when we did, it would be worth the wait.

CHAPTER 12
TWEEDLEDO AND TWEEDLEDON'T

We didn't have to jump over a brook to make it into the fourth square. The train did the jumping for us, soaring through the air and throwing us out at the edge of a forest. I wasn't looking forward to going in there – Alice had lost her memory of even her name in this part of the book – but with Jake beside me, we nattered easily while we walked. We kept on holding hands, too, with no discussion about it.

When we came to two signposts, both pointing in the same direction, we were jolted back to reality. 'They're supposed to say *Tweedledum* and *Tweedledee*, right?' said Jake. 'Only...'

Only they didn't. One sign said *Tweedledo* and the other *Tweedledon't*. The writing on the signs was messy, as though it had been smeared on by the finger of a crazy person. It was done in a brownish-red, and it smelled faintly metallic.

'You don't think...' Jake trailed off with a shiver.

'That they're vampires? I mean, almost everything else has been, even the Cheshire Cat. But whether they're vamps or not, it shouldn't make a difference, should it? They're just some weirdo brothers who'll want to put on silly costumes and fight over a rattle or something like they did in the book.'

'Yeah. Yeah, it'll be easy,' said Jake, not sounding completely convinced. He squared his shoulders and said, 'Let's go.'

I noticed, as we walked towards the clearing where the house was, that Jake stayed slightly in front, his whole body on alert as we moved. He finally let go of my hand, but only so he could take this more protective position. I didn't know what *either* of us could do if things went wrong – we didn't have any magic in here, after all – but his actions made me feel as though he was ready for anything.

When we came upon Tweedledo and Tweedledon't, they were sitting on a porch in matching rocking chairs. The men were nearly identical, even in their clothing – both wore stiff white shirts and black trousers – but one had *Don't* embroidered on his collar, while the other had *Do*.

For a moment they just rocked back and forth on their creaking chairs, looking disinterestedly at us. After a while, one of them said, 'I say we get this over with and recite *the Walrus and the Carpenter,* like Her Majesty wants us to do.'

The other smiled slyly and licked his lips. 'Well, *I* say we don't. Bored of that poem, I am.'

Jake stood tall and square. 'We can hear you, you

know. And if you don't want to recite the poem for us, that's just fine. We know it, anyway. So maybe you could just ask whatever question you have for us, and we'll be on our way.'

Do scratched his chin and said, 'We *could* do that, I suppose.'

'But we don't really want to,' said the other. 'You know how long we've been here?' Before either of us could come up with a reply, he was answering his own question. 'Since the Year of the Raven, that's how long. What's that in years, Do?'

Tweedledo thought about it for a second before saying, 'More than a hundred and twenty years by my calculation, Don't. That's how long Queen Ciara's had this world, with all of us in it. Of course, the last few decades, things haven't been quite as much fun as the earlier years.'

'They haven't,' his brother concurred. 'It was sweet at the beginning, to be sure.' He paused to smile fondly at his horrific memories. 'The Queen of Minds lured in lots of nice morsels back then. But these days, well ... while a vampire might be able to *live* on the stuff the Rabbit Guard courier in, it doesn't give us the same vim and vigour. We're sick of Ciara's promises of breaking us all out of here. We're sick of playing her games, and pretending to be two dumb idiots fighting over a rattle. So *I* say we fight the girl to the death, instead – or stick her in a cage and rattle *her* for a while. You know – tenderise her before we chow down.'

As he spoke, they both leapt towards me, moving so

quickly I didn't see a thing until they were on me, dragging me up onto the porch.

Jake sprang into action, nocking one of his arrows with a speed and grace that blew me away. Then, with a growl in his voice worthy of Fee, he said, 'Oh yeah? Well *I* say you don't. I'm an excellent aim, and like you say – it's been a long time since the two of you ate properly. Which means whatever vampire strength you once had is long, long gone. So get your hands off my Annie, or you'll never see twilight again.'

There was something about the look in his eyes that made them shrink away and loosen their hold, and something about the way he said *'my Annie'* that made my chest expand with breath. I staggered towards Jake, my eyes drinking him in.

And Laine had said Jake was *wet*. Hah! If he could see him now.

Eyes on the weirdo twins, we backed out of their clearing and into the woods.

'Something happens here, doesn't it?' Jake murmured, once we were safely away. 'I feel like I remember ... something ...'

'We meet the White Queen next, I think,' I said. 'No, no, you're right. Something else happens first. I think the air's making my brain sluggish again, though, because I'm struggling to remember. A ... a bird, maybe? Oh! There it is!' I pointed to the darkening sky. 'A huge crow – but it just makes a hurricane, I think, in the book. It doesn't do much more than that, does it?'

The crow was so large that it took out what little light had penetrated the woods. We were in pitch black now. It was so dark that I felt, rather than saw, what happened next: a strong wind, as the crow flapped its wings and flew down, fast; a tug against my shoulder, and a cry, as Jake was whipped off his feet and snatched away.

It wasn't until the sky lightened again that I saw him, far, far above me, clutched in the enormous crow's talons, kicking and hitting out at it while he shouted down to me: 'Keep going, Annie! Don't worry about me! I'll find you!'

CHAPTER 13
A SPELL OF MY OWN INVENTION

I wished so hard that someone or something would appear out of the blue to help us. If only my Griffin – or even the Wonky Wonderland Gryphon – would fly to the rescue and grapple Jake away from the crow.

But after a few brief seconds of hoping and praying, I realised that all I was doing was wasting time. This was a world of Ciara's creation. A bleak and irritating world. And in such a world, no one was coming to save us.

Jake's quiver of arrows and his bow had been knocked to the ground when he was taken, so I picked both up and ran through the undergrowth, keeping my eyes on the sky.

Every now and then I spotted the crow, but it flew so fast that I couldn't really focus on it before it had gone again. Maybe it was just as well – knowing *my* aim, I'd probably hit Jake instead of the bird.

Soon, they were completely out of my sight.

He'd told me to keep going, so I did – I had no choice, really, if we wanted to get out of here alive. But without Jake by my side, this world felt creepier and more annoying than ever. I staggered through the red-orange twilight from one point to the next, interacting with Ciara's version of the book's characters, going through the motions and not marvelling at a single thing.

The first character I encountered alone was the White Queen, who talked in nonsense before finally asking me her question. Funnily enough, it was similar to what Hugo said just as this whole mess began: 'How many impossible things must one believe before breakfast?'

'Six,' I replied wearily.

Things carried on in a dreamy, bizarre style, just as they did in the books. The Queen turned into a sheep, and I next found myself in a shop, and then on a rowboat clutching at reeds, then back in the same shop again...

Not for the first time today, I felt as though I'd eaten one of Windflower's special jellies. But somehow, I advanced across the chessboard countryside, drifting into a meeting with Humpty Dumpty, after which I endured an encounter with the White King, along with all of his horses and all of his men (come to put Humpty together again?).

I smiled and nodded and persevered, answering one *Alice*-based question after the next, as I met the king's strange messengers, and the Lion and the Unicorn who fought for a crown. The Unicorn did threaten to eat *me* instead of some plum cake, but even that moment wasn't too dicey. I simply chucked the cake tin at him and dashed away, and he didn't attempt to follow.

Hugo once told me unicorns were overrated. He was correct.

By the time I heard the thundering of hooves, I'd lost count of what square I was in. I snapped to attention as a knight came galloping up behind me, dressed in crimson and carrying a great big club.

'Ahoy there, little lady! Check!' he roared. 'You're my prisoner now!'

'Ah, I see.' I stepped out of his way before he could grab me and hoist me onto his horse. 'Just ... gimme a minute, will you?' I surveyed the land around me, wondering where my White Knight was. Alice's had arrived at this point in the story.

Just as I was beginning to worry, he appeared, galloping across the countryside to fight the Red Knight and rescue me. I waited patiently while they fought, watching as they knocked each other on the head and whacked their clubs about. Somehow – the rules were about as unclear to me as anything else in this place – it was decided that the White Knight was the winner.

He agreed that he wouldn't take me prisoner, saying he would see me through to the edge of the square instead. Everything was happening according to the book, just as I'd thought it would, but ... somehow, I hadn't expected the White Knight to have such a lovely shape, or voice. Muffled though he was by the visor, I *knew* the man behind that voice.

'You're no White Knight,' I said. 'You're Jake. But ...

how are you here? Last I saw, you were taken by that giant crow. Did the Queen of Minds force you to play a character?'

'Who is this Jake?' he questioned, hopping lithely to the ground. 'I am your White Knight, and you are my Alice. Come, Alice, we have much ground to cover.'

'Not Alice.' I shook my head sadly. 'Annie.'

'Well then, glorious maiden Annie. Let me assist you in mounting, and then I shall ride with you and make you my Queen.'

Quelling the need to fan myself, I let him lift me onto the horse. For a while, after I first met Sir Blake Bingley, I'd been a woman of two fantasies, spending an equal amount of my daydreaming hours imagining scenarios with either of the two: Jake taking me for picnics, or Sir Bingley (via some sort of time travel spell) coming to the museum and saying, 'Fair maiden Annie, can we go on a date sometime?'

Lately, since I'd found out that Jake was single, my Sir Bingley fantasies had taken a back seat. Now, though, I was being lifted onto a horse by my two daydreams combined: Jake, dressed in armour, looking ever so dashing.

Once I was comfortably seated he got up behind me, his arms wrapping around me as his hands took the reins.

Jake might have no idea he was Jake, but I was under no such illusion. There was no mistaking his scent: paint and turpentine and some citrussy soap. And there was certainly no mistaking the way he made me feel.

Ciara had gotten into his mind, somehow, making him think he was a character from the book. He played the part well, telling me all about his crazy inventions, just as the book's White Knight had told Alice.

After a while it grew hot again, and as he took off his helmet I held my breath, waiting for his face to be revealed. I broke out into a broad grin when I saw it – I'd *known* it was Jake behind that armour, but seeing his eyes again filled me up with joy.

We'd travelled some distance when we heard a rumbling sound behind us – not hooves, though. This was much too loud to be another knight on a horse.

I looked behind and saw something running after us. I couldn't make out much at this distance except for the long, long legs, the huge head and the snapping jaws – some might even call them frumious.

'It's a Bandersnatch!' Jake cried, urging the horse into a gallop. 'We'll hide in the woods till he passes!'

The creature was so fast I thought for sure it would be upon us in a flash, but Jake rode harder and harder, taking us under the cover of the trees. There, he and his horse crept their way through until we reached an area so dense we couldn't go any further.

'Our mount will stay here,' Jake announced, leaping gracefully to the ground and reaching out to help me down. 'You and I shall journey a little deeper into the woods. I must keep you out of sight of the Bandersnatch – after all, it's you that it wants.'

'Me?' I questioned. 'Why does it want me?'

He blinked at me, his eyes clouding over with confusion. 'I do not know. But ... I know I am not to let it get you.' He paused in the shade of an enormous oak. 'Here is as good a spot as any but ... who knows what lengths this creature will go to? Perhaps I should make us both invisible. I have a spell that can do that very thing.'

'A spell? Jake, our magic doesn't work in this world.'

'Ah, but my spell is not *of* this world. It is a spell of my own invention, from another world. A world which lurks in the recesses of my mind. A misty memory of a terrible place filled with terrible people. People who frightened me. I was trapped with them in a realm of shimmering bars.'

'Shimmering bars?' I looked up into his eyes. They were filled with pain and sorrow. 'That sounds like ... like Witchfield Prison. Jake, you're remembering your real life, not the White Knight's.'

He shook his head. 'Please, it hurts my head so when you call me Jake. I know not who he is. All I know is that I was scared there. And, like here, it was a world where the usual spells would not work to protect me. So, I made a spell that was not a spell. A magic that was not magic. Whenever I was most frightened, most at risk, I willed myself to disappear, to be unseen. So please, let me hold you, and I will make us both fade away.'

Sympathy poured through me, making tears spring to my eyes. *That* was why Jake faded in and out as much as he did. It had become second nature to him in Witchfield, to make himself go unnoticed, to protect himself from the prison bullies he was trapped with, while he served a sentence for a crime he didn't commit.

Swallowing, I let him put his arms around me and

back me up against the trunk of the oak. My heart thumped wildly, and my body tingled all over, as he began to fade before my eyes. Soon, I could no longer see his sandy hair, his brown eyes. The freckles across his nose and cheekbones were the last things to vanish. And somehow, enveloped in his magic that wasn't magic, I saw my own body fade away, too. Even the strand of hair which had been in my eyeline – all of me was gone, lost in Jake's arms.

'I don't think I've ever been so sad to see someone's face disappear,' he said, a wistful note in his voice. I felt him reach out to me, tracing my jawline, my cheekbone. A sort of fever came over me at his touch, and I found myself reaching out too, tracing the bones of his face just as he traced mine.

'I think I know you,' he whispered hoarsely. 'And I think I like you so, so much. Do we ... are we...?'

'Not yet,' I whispered back. 'But I would really, really like to be.'

I felt his face move closer to mine. I felt his breath, hot. And even though, somewhere in the distance, the Bandersnatch roared, I didn't feel any fear. I just let my head tilt back, let Jake's lips find mine, and allowed myself to sink into bliss.

I don't know how long we'd been that way, lost in kisses, when a hissing sound made us jump. With a groan of reluctance, I opened my eyes and looked around. I couldn't see anything much, so I looked at Jake instead. Now, I could see all of him again, every inch of his face, right down to his amazing mouth. I could see my own body again, too. Maybe it was a trick of the light, but I thought that my skin shimmered, just a little, and that Jake's face and eyes shimmered too.

'Stop giving him the googly-eyes, will you, Annie?' said a voice I recognised. Soon after he spoke, the rest of him grew visible on a branch just above us: a sharp-toothed grin appeared first, followed swiftly by a furry face, pointy ears, and a chubby marmalade body.

'Cheshire Cat,' I said with a grunt of irritation. 'What do you want?'

The cat sighed forlornly. 'Oh, it's *way* too late for what I want. You've just gone through the motions, haven't you? Played her game. Like a chump.'

He wasn't wrong about that. 'What else could we do, though?' I questioned.

'Listened to me at the start. Still ... I'll see you again soon. And Fee is fine, in case you're wondering. Though it looks like you might've forgotten all about her.'

I stared at him, about to ask him *so* much more, but he vanished again. He'd taken any tingles of romance along with him. Now, all I felt was a shiver of fear and realisation.

'I think ... I think he might be on our side,' I said with a gasp. 'I think we should have listened to him earlier on, when we met him near the March Hare's house. When he said we were better off with a Bandersnatch than with the Queen. This whole game, everything Queen Ciara said ... I *know* it's a trap, all of it. I wish I could just ... just think more clearly. But it's like the cat said – I've just been going through the motions, like I'm a character in someone else's dream. I should have taken control. But I didn't.'

Jake turned away and grunted. 'I know nothing of what you speak. All I know is that I need to get you to the crossing for the Eighth Square.'

He left the tree, stomping around in his heavy armour as he searched for the horse, and with a leaden feeling in my belly, I followed.

I felt so, so sad, and I wasn't even sure why. Because what had I really expected? For our kiss to fully jog his memory? For him to act like Jake again, instead of the White Knight?

I didn't even know *my* mind in here, that much was clear. Otherwise I would have tried to talk to the people I met – talk to them *properly,* discover Ciara's real plan, find a way to rescue my friends, and Dora, and get us all home. But the Queen of Minds had been controlling my every move, had been clouding my thoughts, all along.

That kiss, though ... that was real. That was Jake. At least I hoped so.

Once we found the horse we rode along together slowly, sitting as close as we could sit, not saying a word. Maybe Jake didn't know who he was, and maybe I *still* couldn't think as clearly as I'd like, but we both knew one thing: being this close, it was a feeling that neither of us wanted to end.

When we arrived at the brook that separated us from the final square, he sat there for a good half a minute, his face buried in my hair, before dismounting and helping me down.

'I can't go with you,' he said, his hands lingering on my waist. They were cold, on account of the armour, but I didn't care.

'I guess not,' I agreed. 'But this game is pretty much over, so I'll see you again very soon. I hope.'

'I would wish that more than anything,' he said. 'I shouldn't ask this, but ... one more kiss, and then I'll go?'

'One more kiss,' I murmured, wrapping my arms around his neck and pulling him close.

CHAPTER 14
QUEEN ANNIE

When Jake finally left me and galloped away, I stood looking after him for a long, long while. I knew I had some choices now. I could track down the Cheshire Cat – or better yet, a Bandersnatch. Maybe if I did that I could get some answers, and possibly even take control.

Or I could finish the game, just like I feared Ciara wanted me to, and face what was coming next.

Instead of making up my mind, though, I was thinking about Jake. About those kisses. I could still taste him, smell him.

But once we got home, what then? Would he be forced to forget every moment?

Trying to shake away the pointless thoughts, I scanned the area. There was no Bandersnatch in sight now, and no sign of the cat, either. I called out, 'Cheshire Cat! Here, kitty, kitty!' a few times over, but he never materialised.

I finally gave up and jumped the brook, floating over

it in the dreamlike way I'd grown used to in this world, but I had no idea whether I did it because I wanted to, or because Ciara made me.

When I landed in the Eighth Square it seemed smaller than the other squares. It was simply a strip of soft, mossy grass, very nearly empty except for an archway with a door in the middle and a bell on either side. In the book, one bell had been labelled *Visitors' Bell* and the other *Servants' Bell*. Alice had been irritated at that, because she felt sure she was a queen by then, so neither option seemed to fit.

But Alice had a crown at this point, whereas I didn't, which meant ... what? Had I lost the game, somehow, despite making it to the Eighth Square?

I knocked at the door, but unlike in the book, no creature answered it, and there was no frog sitting under a nearby tree. There was just me, and the two bells – and even those were not the same as Alice's.

One bell read: *Wanna Get the Heck out of Here? If so, pull me and say,* 'Ding Dong.' The other bore the words: *Wanna Be a Queen? If so, pull me and say,* 'Dong Ding.'

Oh, how I wished all four of us were here, and we'd somehow managed to grab Dora, too. Then I would *definitely* choose the first bell and get the heck out of here. But it was too late now. Even the cat had said so. If I was going to get the others back, I feared I had no choice but to ring the second bell. But before I did, I got the bow and an arrow at the ready, hoping to the goddess that I could actually shoot it if necessary. I then used my mouth to tug at the bell, mumbling, 'Dong Ding,' as I pulled.

The door shot open, and I walked through cautiously,

looking all around me, wishing I felt a little more badass with the bow and arrow in hand. Instead, I felt clumsy, shaky and likely to trip over my own feet.

It only took me as long as it would take to walk through any doorway, and yet I emerged miles away, back in the March Hare's garden, where another tea party was taking place (or, quite possibly, the exact same one was still going on).

The Queen of Minds was sitting at the head of the table, with the Knave on one side and the Duchess on the other. Other guests were seated, twelve in total with one seat free, while many more stood huddled all around the garden, watching on. Some were creatures we'd met along the way, others were characters we'd managed to circumvent to save time.

Hugo and Jake were at the table, but there was no Fee. Jake was now in his everyday clothes, looking dazed, and Hugo was back in his manly form but letting out the odd, 'Oink!' There were holes in his suit where the pig-wings had poked through. Knowing Hugo, that would annoy him more than anything that had happened today.

I wondered why neither of them got up, and then I realised: they were tied to their chairs.

'Now would be a great time for you to make an appearance, ghost-man,' I muttered, trying desperately to feel any sort of power coming from my locket. But there was nothing.

Jake's eyes met mine. He flushed slightly, and so did I, and then a slow, gorgeous smile crept across his face, a smile that made me sure that – for now, at least – he remembered our kisses.

The March Hare was buttering a watch (as you do), while the Hatter was once again attempting to squash Dora into the teapot. She was complaining dozily and, seeing me, her eyes widened with fright.

'Take a seat, Annie,' said the Queen, indicating the chair in between Hugo and Jake. 'We're all about to have a nice cup of tea. I did think about greeting you at the Eighth Square and testing you on your addition, subtraction, and whether you knew the French for fiddle-de-dee – just so we could stay vaguely on theme. But I had your party to prepare.'

She took Dora out of the pot and began to pour. Somehow, the small pot contained enough to fill thirteen cups, which were laid at each place by Mr White. The liquid looked steaming hot, and yet Dora appeared unharmed – she wasn't even the slightest bit wet or bedraggled.

'Where's Fee?' I demanded, standing firm.

'Ah yes. The wolf who thinks she's not a wolf.' Queen Ciara pointed to the sky. 'As you can see, I've gotten rid of the full moon.'

I couldn't see, actually, because there was no way I was going to look up at that sky and take my eyes off Ciara, even for a second.

'She should be returning to herself presently,' she continued. 'I've left some clothing for her on a washing line at the edge of the forest – it's an exact replica of the outfit she destroyed during the change.'

'How very kind of you,' I said, training my arrow at

the centre of her chest. 'But I know this is a trap. I know you *wanted* me to win that game of chess – if you can even call it that. And I did. I may not have a crown on my head, but I got to the Eighth Square just like Alice did, which by the rules of that book makes me a queen. So we're going to play things my way for a change. Untie my friends and let them come over to me – Dora, too.'

'Don't forget the teapot!' Hugo cried out, then looked away from me, blushing with embarrassment. 'Never mind.'

'No, actually, Hugo, you're right,' I said. 'We were promised that if I played that game I would get to leave here with Dora, all of my friends, *and* the teapot. So I suggest you do as you promised, Ciara. If not, I'm going to shoot this arrow through your heart.'

Ciara laughed, and at first I thought it was because she could see right through my bravado. But I soon realised that, while I'd been speaking, the bow and arrow had been growing softer. By the time I noticed, my weapon had almost entirely crumbled to dust.

Before I could react, three White Rabbit Guards lunged for me, dragging me to the table and pinning me to the empty chair. They didn't look happy about it, but they were doing it anyway. Next time I met the faery queen, I might suggest that her chosen guards were *not* the best for the job.

I looked helplessly at Jake and Hugo. Guards were untying their ropes, but at the same time they were pressing down on them so strongly that neither of my friends could move. These rabbity men might look kind of silly, but they were uncannily strong.

Dora made a beeline for my lap, curling up into a shivering ball once she got there. The Queen and the rest of the guests took up a loud, strange song:

> *'Inside Wonky Wonderland, Annie did say:*
> *"I've a crown on my head now, this is my day*
> *Let the Queen's creatures, whatever they be*
> *Come to tea at this table, with royals,*
>   *with me."*
> *Change places! Sing chorus!'*

At the end of that verse, everybody moved to the next seat along, singing the chorus as they went. I didn't *want* to move, neither did Jake and Hugo, but the rabbity men yanked us into the next chairs despite all of our kicking and screaming.

> *'Drink of the teapot as quick as you can*
> *Now Dora's magic will still Annie's hand*
> *Oh Dora, oh Dora, the mouse in the tea*
> *It's always been you who brings Annie to me!'*

As the chorus died out, the Queen cried, 'Change places!' once more. On and on we went, the others singing more verses, repeating that same chorus, moving seats again and again, until eventually I was sitting at the head of the table.

The Queen gave me a long, lingering smirk, and then she yanked a hair from Mr White's moustache and threw it at the ground. As a rabbit hole opened up, she, the Duchess and the Knave jumped into it and vanished.

'What's happening, Dora?' I asked, feeling a heavy weight on my head. Touching it, I could feel that it was a crown. I tried to take it off, but it wouldn't budge.

'You're this realm's monarch now, Annie. Which means that Ciara ... she's free. But it's all going to be okay. Help is coming.' She looked to the horizon, where a dozen Bandersnatches were running towards us, led by a large, snarling werewolf. And sitting atop the werewolf's back, clearly enjoying the ride, was the Cheshire Cat.

CHAPTER 15
A TALE OF TAILS

I soon discovered something interesting about Bandersnatches: the closer they get, the harder they are to see. As they neared me their bodies grew blurry, out of focus, so that all I could really get a good look at was their jaws – funnily enough, those jaws didn't seem nearly as frumious anymore.

I might have been the only one who felt that way, though, because at the sight of the newcomers, even the most frightening of the Queen's creatures slinked away (Tweedledo and Tweedledon't actually ran). It was just us, then – Jake, Hugo, Dora and me – waiting worriedly for Dora to speak, and for Fee and her new gang to approach.

I could sense, though, that it could be a while before Dora's nerves calmed down. It was as if the connection I felt with her had suddenly grown about a million times stronger. In the past, I'd sometimes been certain she was my familiar, but other times in doubt of that. Now, I knew without reservation that she was mine and I was hers. I could feel so much love coming from her that it sort of blew me away. It felt as though I'd just discovered a limb I'd never known I was missing. A sleepy, fluffy limb with the cutest ears and tail.

Fee paused about twenty feet away from us, to let the Cheshire Cat jump down. He moved swiftly to the washing line and deftly grabbed the clothing before delivering it to Fee. She disappeared behind a bush, then – presumably to get changed (in more ways than one). Even though she was well hidden, Hugo made extra, extra sure to avert his eyes.

The shock had made us all a bit slow of thinking, because it took us a while to realise that, without the rabbity men here to hold us down, we could now move freely. Jake ran to my side, tenderly touching my cheeks and looking into my eyes. 'You okay?'

I nodded, swallowing down all the things I wanted to say (and do), and said, 'Yeah, fine, apart from this big heavy crown that seems to be stuck on my head. You guys?'

'Me and Hugo are good,' said Jake, flashing his eyes to Hugo, as Hugo let out another *oink*. 'Well ... good-*ish*. The oinking is bound to taper off with time, right? And we're a little confused and mixed-up, but...'

He bit his bottom lip shyly and, lowering his voice, added, 'I might not have acted like myself the whole time I was the White Knight, but now that it's over I remember it all. And I know this maybe isn't the ideal time, but I might just explode if I don't tell you – well, that I don't regret a second of it.'

'Me neither,' I said, my lashes (and my stomach) going ever so fluttery.

Fee, now back to her usual self and dressed in a lemon-yellow dress and matching hat, was walking towards us. Judging by the cheeky smirk on her face, her super-ears allowed her to hear *all* of that. She was cuddling the Cheshire Cat in her arms (he, for his part, was purring and preening under her touch). The band of Bandersnatches sat down on their haunches a few feet from the table, panting and smiling and looking adoringly at Fee.

'You okay?' I asked her.

'Thanks to this little kitty and his Bandersnatch buddies. They sought me out, made sure I got something to eat and helped me wait out the full moon without doing any damage. They even found my wand and brought it to me, which is a relief, because I can't afford to replace it. I thought it was lost for good after I wolfed out, but apparently not.' She cast an awe-filled look at the Bandersnatches. 'Those guys seem to communicate quite well with animals, but not so well with people. They're surprisingly lovely. Who would've thunk it, eh? They're agents of the fae queen – the one who imprisoned Ciara here. This cute little guy is an agent, too – he's been back and forth between me and you guys for hours, checking up on us.' She paused to kiss the cat's head.

'The flowers in the garden we saw when we arrived, they work for the fae queen too,' she continued. 'They mainly act as spies – telling the fae queen who comes and goes. She made a few Wonky Wonderland residents an offer some years ago. But ... maybe you should tell them this bit, Chesh.'

The Cheshire Cat purred and nodded. 'Ciara, the Knave and the Duchess are the worst offenders in this prison, followed by Tweedledo and Tweedledon't,' he informed us. 'Many others, like me, were told we could shorten our stays here if we complied with the faery queen. Dora was offered total freedom, being that the faery queen could sense she was totally innocent. But because of the bonding spell with Ciara, Dora swore that she was as much a part of Ciara's shenanigans as anyone else. She didn't have a choice. Did you, D?'

Dora looked down at her front paws, shivering but saying nothing.

'It's been harder for Dora than any of us,' the Cheshire Cat went on. 'But that's not to say it's been a walk in the park for those of us who took the faery queen up on her offer. Within this place, Ciara's sway is strong. Half of the time she's inside our heads, fiddling about with our thoughts and even our actions. But we try. As for the Bandersnatches, they've always worked for the faery queen. They work as prison patrol, and back up the White Rabbit Guard if there's a dicey situation. They're to keep an eye out for anyone wandering in by accident, too, and chase them down. Under normal circumstances, they'd hand people like you over to the White Rabbit Guard, who would then bring you to the faery queen so she could sort things out.'

'But these are not normal circumstances,' I said with a sigh. 'The guards have been working for the Queen of

Minds instead. But – that means that Ciara's escaped by now.'

'No, it doesn't,' said Dora, finally speaking up. 'That's what she's aiming to do, yes. But unless you're a member of the Rabbit Guard, a whisker can only help you travel *within* this world. Ciara's rabbit hole will take her and her evil friends to the garden you lot encountered when you first entered. And given there are many more Bandersnatches, and the garden is already filled with the faery queen's agents, it's safe to say they'll be delayed. We have time for me to – well, to explain everything.' She paused to let out a yawn. 'Because I actually *can,* now. Something happened when you swapped places with her, Annie. The false bond I shared with Ciara is completely gone.'

Her words explained what I was feeling – the sudden strength of the connection, the absolute certainty that we belonged to each other. The overwhelming sense of love.

'So what *did* Ciara tell you guys when she whisked you off to play croquet?' Dora questioned. 'I'm guessing it was a version of the truth, but with one or two holes.'

Jake and I filled her in as best we could about the Queen's tale, and the task she'd set us.

'Yeah,' said Dora when we'd finished. 'That's what I thought she'd say. It's true that I one day felt a *real* bond with you, Annie, when I saw you through the mirror. And our bond helped you open the portal and come through. It's also true that I watch you, and do my best to look out for you, and that I've sometimes been able to travel to your world myself.'

My eyes were stinging as she spoke. 'And if I'd been certain enough of our bond, you could have stayed there, with me.'

With a great deal of fervour, she shook her head. 'No. No, that part is *not* true.'

'But you said so yourself – you told me it was important I believed that you were my familiar.'

'Oh, it is – and we'll come to that later. But you need to know, Annie, there was absolutely nothing you could have done to keep me in your world, not as long as Ciara kept me on a magical leash.' She let out another yawn and added, 'My natural bond with you was strong enough to circumvent the false bond sometimes, but never to override it.'

'But still, I *could* have gotten you out of here, years ago,' I argued. 'Ciara said that when Hugo and I came here as kids, I could have taken you home if we'd won the game. Except I failed.'

'Another lie. You *won,* Annie. You got to the Eighth Square, you and Hugo both.'

'We did, Annie,' Hugo agreed, his voice a mere whisper. 'But Ciara wanted more, back then. That's what I remembered before I was turned into a pig. She cheated you then, just like she cheated you now. The game of chess was a spell to help her escape.'

'Yes,' said Dora. 'It was. But it was only part of the spell. Making this place, running this place, and trying to *escape* this place ... all of it is possible with the right kind of spell. A spell which Ciara and the Duchess know, and which cannot be conducted without me.'

'You?' I gawped at her. 'You helped *make* this place?'

'Not willingly,' said Dora. 'But yes. You see, I'm related to *the* Dormouse. The one who lives in the real Wonderland. In Lewis Carroll's book, Alice argued with my relative. She pulled him up on bits of his story.'

'The story of the sisters who lived in a treacle-well,' said Jake with a smile. 'Alice thought they'd be ill if they ate nothing but treacle.'

'Precisely,' Dora confirmed. 'But in reality, Alice would have believed every word he said, because he, and I – like most in our family – have the gift of the gab. I can tell a story so convincing that it sways people – even the strongest of vampires would struggle to match me. And my powers combined with Ciara's, *and* with my teapot ... that's how the Duchess and Ciara were able to create this place, and how they managed to control it.'

I looked at her in amazement. 'Your teapot?'

'Yes. Mine. Every magical dormouse has one – though I personally prefer to snooze in a cup. A tea made in a dormouse's pot, in a certain way, can make virtually anything possible. We can spin a completely believable tale – with some help, of course, from our magical tails.' She let out a sleepy giggle. 'Or with a little bit of the fluff from our tails, anyhow, added to the mixture. I'm not sure if it's just accident that our magic concentrates at that part of our bodies, or if we somehow evolved like this because we like puns so much. Either way, my magic made Ciara the Queen of Minds at the creation of this world. When she was trapped here, she found a loophole – she could get *out,* as long as she left another Queen of Minds in her place. But the spell has to be done in a very particular way – winning at chess, drinking the tea, and changing places at the table. When you came here twenty years ago, she thought all of her dreams had come true. She intended you to replace her. It didn't work. I convinced her it was because you were too young, but the truth was, the only reason it didn't work was because I spoke to you mind-to-mind, told you to use your power over objects to resist the crown.'

I touched my head. 'I could have resisted this thing?'

'You could. But it was harder for me to communicate with you today. Maybe because Ciara made sure that our false bond was super-strong this time around, or maybe because you didn't have your wand. You probably don't remember, but you had a hawthorn wand when you were a little girl, Annie. There was something special about it. It protected you, somehow. Your magic was intact the whole time you were here, because of it, and Ciara never once got into your mind. It didn't just get the two of you safely to the Eighth Square. It's as if it calmed you down and helped you focus your magic, too. You were even able to stop the Duchess from turning Hugo into a pig.'

On cue, Hugo oinked. With a beet-red face, he said, 'Why did she do that to me?'

Dora shrugged. 'She's always messing about with things that are perfectly fine as they are. But Annie, back then you were able to control that crown the way you can control all magical objects, even though you were only seven, and your powers were pretty new and mostly unknown to you. I did so hope you'd have the wand this time.'

Hugo's face fell. 'I think Annie *did* have that wand. Or

she would have, if I hadn't gone and chucked it away. I knew I recognised it when I saw it. The wand you've been using all week is your childhood wand, isn't it?'

'I kind of think it might have been,' I said. 'But accidents happen, Hugo. It wasn't your fault. We all had trouble going through the portal.'

'It was my fault, actually,' he told me. 'Something came over me. Made me reach out for it. And then, as I intended to hand it back to you it's like I had this irresistible urge to throw it away. I managed to convince myself it was an accident, but I really don't think it was.'

Dora gave him a gentle smile. 'If you were in the portal, Ciara was probably already in your head. Don't feel bad about it, Hugo.' She hopped from my lap and went over to him, rising up on her back legs so she could reach up and sweetly kiss his nose. 'It wasn't your fault.'

The whole time we'd been speaking, I could feel Fee and Jake looking at me, their curiosity brimming.

'Things are beginning to make a whole lot of sense, now,' said Fee. 'You have this ... way with the artefacts, don't you, Annie? That's why Ralph wants you at the museum. Why you've been helping the Wayfarers out so many times, when it came to Sir Bingley's armour, and the mummy. Heck, it's why Ralph's sent you in here – he thought that with your gifts, you couldn't fail to get that teapot.'

I bowed my head and shrugged. 'Yeah. Yeah, I have some weird magic,' I muttered. 'It's no big deal.'

It was, and they knew it. I could feel it in the way they were looking at me. I wanted to say so much more, but they would only forget it again as soon as we got out of here.

'So, can Annie refuse the crown now?' Jake questioned, looking curiously at Dora. 'Use her power over artefacts to send it back to Ciara? Or maybe – maybe she could pull the tablecloth out, like Alice did in the book. That's how Alice ended the madness, and woke up and went back home.'

'Pulling the tablecloth out would be a very bad idea,' said Dora. 'It *would* have done the trick, originally, but the Duchess redesigned the spell so that, if Annie does that, you'll all be sealed in here for good. And as for the crown, well ... now that it's actually *on* Annie's head, there's technically no way of undoing it.'

The Cheshire Cat grinned. 'Not technically, perhaps. But I'm sensing you have a plan, Dora.'

She gave us all a shy, tentative smile, the kind of smile that made my heart feel warm and fuzzy.

'Twenty years ago,' she said, 'when I told Ciara that the spell mustn't have worked because Annie was too young to take her place, she believed me. She saw Annie as a get-out card and nothing more. She never really grasped how powerful my witch is. And she definitely didn't understand how strong a witch and her true familiar are, united. Otherwise, she never would have left me here with you all. And she certainly wouldn't have left my teapot. But she did. And because of that, we can give this story the ending it deserves.'

CHAPTER 16
THE ENDING IT DESERVES

'The ending it deserves,' said Fee, grinning at Dora. 'I like the sound of that. I also like that I can understand every word you say, even though I'm not a witch. I'm guessing you're working hard to make that happen.'

Dora gave her a small little shrug. 'You spilled your guts to me often enough when you didn't know I was a magical animal. I feel like I owe you.'

Fee cleared her throat. 'Yeah, well, let's not linger on that, will we? Wait – do we actually use your tail fluff to make this tea?'

'She was *in* the teapot for Ciara's spell.' Hugo shuddered. 'I don't understand how you didn't get wet. Or burnt.'

'The tea arrives after I leave the pot,' Dora explained. 'My magic makes it. Or, you can just chuck in a little piece of my fluff and add it to your usual tea – it does much the same job. And we *will* be redoing the spell so things end the way we want, but first...'

She gave me a hopeful look and said, 'First, we need to make sure that even on the off-chance Ciara and her pals get past the Bandersnatches, Ciara can't get out. Because if she does, it won't be long before she opens up this entire realm again, and *everyone* will escape. Ciara and her cronies in the real world, well ... *that* story won't end well. So to make sure it doesn't come to that, Annie, you need to use your power in a stronger way than you've ever used it before. You need to connect with the portal mirror, and tell it not to let Ciara through.' Sensing I was about to interrupt, she gave me a no-nonsense stare and added, 'And yes, you *can* control the mirror.'

'No, I can't,' I argued. 'The portal closed behind us the second we arrived.'

'It didn't, actually,' Dora informed me. 'Ciara must've got into your head the same way she got into Hugo's, because believe me when I tell you, you *can* control it. How do you think the mirror turned back into a portal in the first place?'

'Our bond?' I said weakly.

'Not quite. Our bond made you *want* to open it back when you came here first. And our bond continued to make you want me, even when you didn't remember me, so that I was able to journey through from time to time. But actually getting the portal to work? I mean, come on – you don't actually think that someone as powerful as the faery queen simply forgot to close up a portal into this place, do you? No way, Jose – it was fully shut, just like all the others. Until *you* came along.'

'Yes, but ... I had my wand then,' I said. 'And my magic. I don't have either now.'

She hopped back into my lap. 'You're Queen of Minds now, which means you get to decide who does and doesn't have magic in this place. So get in touch with your magic, and use it. And I know you think you can't, so *this* is the part I was talking about, Annie – the part where you need to believe I'm your familiar. Because as long as you believe in me, I can help you feel your magic, enhance your magic.' She let out an impatient sigh. 'Okay, pep talk over. Let's do this thing, and quick.'

There was a small, insecure part of me that wanted to carry on arguing, insisting that I couldn't possibly do what she seemed to think I could. But today, I would have to put my insecurities behind me and just try my best. Otherwise, everyone in the real world would suffer – and everyone who was here with me now would get *very* irritated.

I closed my eyes, touching Dora, reaching out to the Wonky Wonderland around me, and picturing the mirror in my mind. Dora was right. I *could* feel it, I could connect to it, just as strongly as if I was physically touching it. I knew now that it had never wanted to be a portal in the first place, and it had only re-opened because I'd wanted it so much, because I'd sensed Dora, and loved her, even though we were worlds apart.

Well, right now I wanted that mirror to close again – just to Queen Ciara and her minions, mind you.

As I focused harder, I could actually see the mirror – see *out* of it, too, as Ciara, the Knave and the Duchess arrived in the mirror version of Ralph's office. They looked a little the worse for wear, but they were alive.

With her friends to help her, it now seemed inevitable that – unless I could stop it – Ciara *would* get out.

'Stay closed,' I told the mirror, in no uncertain terms. 'Do not let Ciara get out of this realm.'

I watched, through the glass of the mirror, as though I was looking out from its essence, while Ciara jumped at it ... and bounced right back.

'Serves you right, you warped weirdo,' I muttered.

She'd made me believe I was stuck in here. She'd manipulated me every step of the way, using my love for Dora, using my deepest fears, using my friends against me. There was no way I was letting someone like that loose in the real world.

'Okay,' said Dora, smiling brightly, hopping into the teapot. 'That's it. She's trapped. And now, it's time to redo the spell and give ourselves that better ending.' She ran about inside her teapot, her eyes closed firmly. I was much closer to the pot now, able to look into it and see it as she hopped out. As soon as she was gone, it immediately filled up with a golden-brown, steaming tea.

'Whoa.' Jake shook his head, impressed. 'I wish Wim could make his own tea. He's constantly at me to make him a cup.'

'Your familiar drinks *cups* of tea?' Fee lifted a brow. '*Cups?* Not bowls. Isn't he a dog?'

Jake shrugged. 'He is what he is. He likes *some* things in bowls. Strawberries and cream. Broccoli and stilton soup. So what's next, Dora?'

'Next, we sit down to tea – Annie, you need to pour. We don't need to change places for this spell. But we do need to say a rhyme as we drink. Repeat after me:

"Change places," said Ciara
Oh, what a plan
But now Dora's story
Will reverse her hand

Ciara is trapped here
As she always must be
Her crown on her head
She will never be free.'

As we chanted it over and over while drinking the tea (it tasted fizzy and sweet), I felt the crown grow lighter and lighter, until it was whisked right off my noggin. It then went flying through the sky, on its way to rejoin with its rightful owner, at last.

'And now,' said Dora, 'it's time for us all to leave here – that's, you know, if you want to take me. You don't have to. I – I can stay here. It's quite nice, really, at times.'

'You silly eejit.' I kissed the top of her head. 'Prepare to endure the most co-dependant and overbearing relationship ever known, Dora, because I am never letting you out of my sight again.'

She smiled delightedly, and, with a yawn, said, 'I'm looking forward to our unhealthy relationship. We'll keep the shrinks in business for years to come.'

CHAPTER 17
ONE MORE KISS

Fee's gang of Bandersnatches quickly delivered us to the *Looking Glass* section of Ciara's world. I tried my best to study my own Bandersnatch-taxi as he sped me along to my destination, but I still couldn't focus on much but the jaws. It wasn't nearly as psychedelic as my Púca-taxi ride had been, but it sure was fast. Very, very fast. Some of Ciara's characters waved at us as we raced by, while others ran for cover.

We didn't see a single White Rabbit Guard, but they had probably left the world entirely. Ciara might not be able to use their rabbit holes to escape, but as I'd seen in the Museum of Never Again, the rabbity men could definitely use those portals for themselves.

When we arrived at the garden, Ciara and her pals were tied up, surrounded by two dozen Bandersnatches while the flowers looked on, laughing. Fee's twelve Bandersnatches joined the mob, snarling and snapping their jaws at the prisoners. Ciara attempted to say something when she saw us – probably something angry and insulting – but we couldn't hear her above the noise.

Thankfully, our journey back into the tower was a lot quicker than our journey out had been – though we did still float rather than walk up those stairs. When we reached the upstairs landing, Hugo said, 'I remember this bit from before, Annie. From when we were kids.'

I wished I could remember, but I couldn't. Ciara must have been right when she said that Ralph used a stronger memory spell on me than he had on Hugo.

'And you ...' Hugo frowned at Dora. 'You were with us, weren't you? Until–'

Dora blinked, looking down. She'd taken her favourite teacup with her, and she curled up tight inside it. 'Until Ciara caught up with us and grabbed me at the very last second, wrenching me out of Annie's hands just as you guys entered the portal. It was fine, really – even if I *had* made the journey, I would have been pulled back here anyway, because of the false bond.'

I might not remember the moment, but I could remember the feeling, somehow – and it had felt like my heart was shattering apart. 'Never again, Dora – like I said, we're about to have the most suffocating relationship ever known. Although ...' A sudden panic was setting in. 'I've just thought of something. If I'm not Queen of Minds now, I also don't have magic anymore while we're in here, do I? So will I still be able to control the mirror and get us out?'

Dora's bright little eyes rolled theatrically. 'You never stop needing reassurance, do you? Yes, we'll get out. That mirror exists in two places – in this world, and in the museum. And after all of my spying on your progress, I'm fairly sure that every single item in the museum is under your control, right?' She snuggled back down into her cup, adding, 'So, are we going or what?'

We moved to the door, but Fee hesitated at the threshold. 'Actually,' she said, 'I just want to have a private word with Annie for a second, guys, if that's okay.'

Hugo gave her a curious glance, but followed Jake into the office. When Jake politely shut the door, Fee turned to me and said, 'I've seen you use your gifts before, haven't I?'

'Oh, Fee.' I rested back against the wall with a sigh. 'Why are you so bloody clever? Yeah, you have. The museum makes you forget, though. In order to be protected, I had to sign a contract – which means that any time anyone finds out about me, their memories get rewritten. You have to believe me, I am not happy about this, and I'm hoping to find a way around it. There has to be one. Hugo and Ralph get to know, so I don't see why you and Jake can't. You guys are much more part of the museum than Ralph is. And I trust you way more than I trust him. Or Laine.'

'You do?' she asked, spots of colour appearing on her cheeks.

'Of course I do. You were a blooming werewolf, Fee, and yet you managed not to hurt us. That must have been so hard for you. And Hugo, Jake, me, we didn't forget about you for a second. Jake, he went out of his way to find yellow wolfsbane so we could change you back. He em ... he was surprisingly good under pressure.'

'Oh, was he now?' She gave me a teasing smile. 'From what I heard him say, he was your White Knight. How very sexy.'

'I'm not going to lie, Fee – it was *really* hot. But...'

She regarded me perceptively. 'But something special happened between you, and you're worried that he'll forget it all. Look, I hate the thought of forgetting any of this, Annie. Yeah, some of it was terrifying, but a lot of it was amazing, too. The thing is, I'm not sure we *will* forget it all, actually. Think about it – the museum will make Jake and me forget anything to do with your power, right? That's what your contract entails?'

'Yeah, from what I understand.'

'Well then, we'll maybe forget some bits of that last conversation with Dora, and nothing else.' She squeezed my shoulder. 'So whatever it is that happened between you and Jake, this doesn't have to be the end of it.'

'Do you really think so?'

'I absolutely do. But just in case, I think maybe you and he should have a moment before we go.' She let go of me and pushed open the door. 'Jake! Annie wants to talk to you a sec.' Looking down at Dora, she whispered, 'Want to come inside and wait with Aunty Fee for a minute?'

Dora shook her head at me, letting out a breath of faux-outrage, and said, 'I thought we were never to part ways again.' She grinned over at Jake as he walked out into the landing. 'But he *is* a bit of a Cutey McCute Pants, so I guess I'll allow it.'

With that, Fee took Dora into the mirror-office and discreetly shut the door.

Alone with Jake, I had no idea what to say, so thankfully he opened the proceedings, waving shyly and saying, 'Hey.'

I waved back, though we were only about a foot apart. 'Hey.' After a beat or two, I added, 'So, I guess we made it. We're going home.'

'Uh-huh. Can't wait.'

Maybe I was wrong, but I thought I heard a note of reluctance in his voice.

'You don't sound all that enthusiastic,' I told him.

'That obvious?' He crossed his arms, looking anywhere but at me. 'I'm as weird as ever, then. I don't know what's up with me. I mean, okay – maybe I could take or leave the evil vampire queen – and I could *definitely* leave Tweedledo and Tweedledon't. But the rest of it, everything else that happened here ... yeah, there's a part of me that doesn't want to go back.'

'There's a part of me, too,' I said, honestly.

'Right?' He met my eyes, smiling shyly. 'This should have been the worst day ever, instead it's been the best. I wanted ... I didn't want to let you down.'

'You didn't. You were amazing.'

His cheeks flamed. 'So were you. I think that's *why* I didn't want to let you down. You make me feel ... I don't know. Like I never want to disappear again.'

'Oh,' I whispered, just plain gazing at him, unable to tear my eyes away. I knew I should say something more – have the kind of conversation I'd just had with Fee – but I couldn't bear to have that talk with Jake right now.

Couldn't bear to tell him that I had no idea how much of this he'd remember. So instead of saying any of that, I asked, 'Can I have a hug?'

Voice heavy, he said, 'Of course you can.' He moved closer, holding me to his chest, burying his face in my hair.

As he held me, all of my feelings became so *big*. So overwhelming. My heart seemed too immense for my body. It was as though it was trying to burst out and snuggle in with Jake's.

I felt some hope, too, because Fee, with her sharp mind, had figured out something I hadn't. He might not remember all of it, but there was a good chance he'd remember most of it. Maybe we *could* have a relationship. Yes, it might take me some time to figure out how to tell him the full story, and have him retain it all. But the kisses ... there was absolutely no need for him to forget about those.

'What was it I said to you before you headed for the Eighth Square?' he murmured.

I moved my head off his shoulder and looked up at him. '"One more kiss, and then I'll go?"'

He smiled softly. 'Yeah, that,' he said, as he inclined his face to mine.

I felt, for the duration of that kiss, as though my heart *did* burst out and intertwine with his. It couldn't go on forever, though, so after a while we pulled away, and joined our friends at the mirror.

'We should all hold hands,' Hugo suggested. 'Just in case we arrive back in Dad's real office at completely different times.'

'Good idea,' I murmured, dreading our arrival, and what it might bring. But I took a deep breath and held Dora in one hand, clasping Jake's palm with my other. Jake held hands with Fee, and Fee with Hugo, and in Hugo's free hand, he held onto the teapot. He was shivering so much I thought he might drop it, but he somehow managed to keep hold.

'Well?' said Dora, peeping over the rim of her cup. 'What are we waiting for?'

'On three,' said Fee, 'One ... two ... three!'

CHAPTER 18
ENTER SANDMAN

Shortly afterwards, when the mirror let us back through, we found ourselves tumbling to the floor in an empty office. Just as we were standing up and brushing ourselves off (and Hugo was worriedly checking the teapot for signs of damage) Laine strolled into the room, wearing his backpack and whistling a tune.

Seeing us all, he froze for a moment before saying, 'Hugo, Fee, Jake – what are you doing here? Annie and I have work to get on with. We–' His eyes rested on the teapot in Hugo's hands for a moment, and then drifted over to Dora, who was peering over the edge of her cup. 'You – you have a dormouse. And a teapot – *the* teapot. *How?*'

'Because we've just had a very long and tiring visit to Wonkyland. Duh.' Fee rolled her eyes at him. 'Or is it Wonky Wonderland? Anyway, I wouldn't recommend it. Not at this time of year. Far too hazy.'

'But ...' He stared at his watch, and then, as if he

couldn't quite believe it, grabbed my wrist so he could stare at *my* watch instead. 'I've only been gone a few minutes.'

'Oh, didn't you know?' said Hugo, with a smirk. 'Time passes differently in that realm. And I thought *you* were the expert.'

'Some expert,' Fee muttered.

'Oh, I knew,' Laine said. 'I just ...'

A strange look passed over his face, one I couldn't quite read, and before I could react he pulled out a little purse from his pocket. He opened it, brought it up to his lips, and blew, sending a sparkling dust flying first into Jake's face, and then into Fee's.

I watched on in horror as the two of them slumped to the floor, the dust settling all around their bodies for a second, and then fading away.

'What did you do?' I asked, my voice shaking, as I bent down and gently shook them both. They didn't move, didn't respond. They were fast asleep. Jake had a soft smile on his face, while Fee began to snore.

'My job,' Laine said gruffly, moving to Ralph's desk and slamming his hand down hard on the bronze bell. 'It's kind of like Sandman Dust, only while it sends them to sleep, it'll also work on certain memories, and make sure they'll forget everything that happened from the moment they blundered through that mirror.'

I straightened up and glared at him. 'You messed with their *memories*? Isn't it bad enough that the museum already does that to them? They – they would forget anything they might have learned about me, my gift. Why make them forget everything else, too?'

I clutched the cup as I spoke, stroking Dora, trying to calm down, trying not to shout, not to cry. But I really, really wanted to. I wanted to sink to my knees and sob like a little girl. I'd been so hopeful when we jumped back through that portal. Jake and I, we were at the beginning of something. Now ... now it had all been taken from us in a cloud of stupid glittering dust. Horrible things should *not* be sparkly. It was highly misleading.

He squeezed his eyes shut for a moment, then looked at me with huge, apologetic eyes. 'I'm sorry, Annie. I am. But it's what Ralph would want me to do. Trust me – Ralph won't want them remembering anything they learned in that prison world, regardless of whether it's about your gift or not. Hugo'll back me up on that. He knows what his dad's like better than anyone.'

Blinking, Hugo shook his head. 'I ... I ... you have direct communication with my *father*?'

Laine looked guiltily at the bell he'd just rung, then at me.

'You lied to me,' I accused. 'You said you didn't know what that was. You said it was just some knick-knack of Ralph's.'

He held his hands up. 'I know, and I'm sorry. If it was my choice, I would have told you. It's a direct communication device, yes. Part of a pair. Shrinkable, if Ralph and I need to carry them around with us. We only use them in an emergency. I ring, he comes to me as quick as he can, and vice versa. Ralph was afraid if you knew what it was, you'd use it to call him back when you heard about the job.'

I had so much to feel sick about, angry about – I wanted to scream about it all, but I didn't know where I would even begin. In any case, Ralph chose that moment to appear. He was red-faced, wearing a torn travelling cloak and holding a broomstick. His face lost its colour as he looked at us all.

His eyes narrowing at Hugo, he said, 'Would you care to tell me, my dear boy, why there is a werewolf and a souvenir-maker asleep in my office? Hm?' He blinked, then, noticing the teapot, and Dora in her cup. 'But...'

'Yes, Dad. *We* did it,' said Hugo. 'Me, and the werewolf, and the souvenir-maker. We all went to Wonky Wonderland with Annie. It was an accident, but we managed quite well under the circumstances, don't you think? And then your treasure hunter here had to go and blow Sandman Dust in their eyes, because that's *exactly* how this museum ought to reward a job well done. Right?'

While Hugo and his dad were glaring at each other, Jake and Fee began to stir. Fee sat up first, rubbing her head and gazing sleepily around. 'I ... why am I on the floor?' She licked her lips and grimaced. 'And why do I feel like I've swallowed something hairy?'

Jake sat up next to her, looking groggy and confused. 'Oh, man, I don't feel good. My head is thumping, and I ... the last thing I remember, there was a Loony Lunger on the ceiling.' His eyes dashed to mine. 'Did I stop it from biting you, Annie?'

'You did,' I told him with a sad smile. 'You were amazing.'

While Jake blushed, Ralph got down on his

haunches, looking sympathetically at them both. 'As Hugo and Annie were just telling me, the two of *you* got bit by that Loony Lunger. Dear me, I'll bet it's given you one heck of a hallucination.'

'A hallucination? That's one way of putting it,' Jake said with a frown. 'I feel like ... I feel like I've just come back from another world.' His eyes found mine again, and he blushed deeply for a moment, before his face began to fade.

'You two should head home and rest,' Ralph suggested as he straightened up, sounding so incredibly kind and well-meaning that it made me shiver. He was far too good an actor. 'And if you have *any* symptoms, any problems, I'll send the very best healer to see to you both. Can't be too careful with a Loony Lunger bite.'

'But it's not even lunchtime,' said Jake. 'Ralph, you sent me an email to tell me you needed me to start on the glass coffin souvenirs this afternoon. I can't just leave when there's so much work to do.'

'Pah.' Ralph waved a hand and gave Jake a benevolent smile. 'Work can wait, lad. Go on home now and relax, the two of you. Nothing's as important to me as my staff's wellbeing.'

Fee didn't look happy about it – in fact, knowing her as well as I was beginning to, I'd say she was downright suspicious. Nevertheless, she grabbed Jake by the arm and said, 'That's very kind of you, Ralph. We'll head on home.'

CHAPTER 19
DORA'S CHOICE

It was when they were gone that I began to feel frightened. Ralph's eyes devoured the teapot, and then Dora, and it occurred to me: the teapot was no good without the dormouse, or at least without some of her tail fur. He'd wanted them *both*, all along.

She began to shake in her teacup, and I kissed her head softly and said, 'Well, I'll be off. We've been hours in there. I'm knackered.'

I tried to sound ever so nonchalant as I made my way to the door, but Ralph was standing there, blocking my path. 'Not so quick, Annie. I'd like a detailed report, if you don't mind, of everything that happened in that prison world. You too, Hugo. Stay here and fill your old father in, won't you? Like a good boy.'

For a few seconds, Hugo looked at me instead of his dad. The expression in his eyes was pleading, as though he hoped I'd have some magical solution. But I didn't even have my magical wand. I thought about sidestepping Ralph and making a run for it, but what then? He could easily catch me, or freeze me. I couldn't let him have Dora, not after everything I'd been through to bring her home, but ... how could I stop him?

'Okay,' Hugo said, sounding resigned. 'I'll give you a report.'

As he began to tell our tale, I felt so sorry for him. He might never admit it – he might even lie and call it respect – but it was clear that he feared his father as much as I did.

Laine was quiet throughout, looking just as miserable and resigned as Hugo, and I felt a little sorry for him, too. I felt sorry for all of us, really. But under that sorrow I was seething, thinking, trying to come up with some way – any way – to get Dora out.

Hugo had just gotten to the part about the croquet game when he stopped abruptly, his eyes lighting up as he lunged under his dad's desk. He emerged a moment later with a triumphant smile on his face, and my wand in his hand. 'It's not lost, Annie! When Ciara made me chuck it out of the portal, it must have landed right here!'

He looked deeply relieved, and I was too. The wand was shining with that lovely white light, completely fine and intact. I was about to cross the room and take it from him, when Ralph cleared his throat in the most annoying of ways, and said, 'That wand is museum property, son. The teapot too. Just hand them to me and we'll say no more about it.'

For a second, I thought Hugo was about to do it. He leaned forward, held them out, but then he suddenly jerked back, looking angrier than I'd ever seen him look. 'No. No, I won't. This is Annie's wand. I remember now. I remember waking up that day, all those years ago. I was in one of our storerooms, next to Annie, after we got back from Queen Ciara's world the first time around, and *you* were looming over us when we woke. Annie was disoriented after the memory spell you used on her. And you – you took advantage. You plucked her wand from her hand and said it was yours, and she was too confused to argue. You tricked a *child*. Why?'

When Ralph declined to answer, Laine said, 'I think I can guess why. He wanted to examine it, right? To see if it was a portal key. When it wasn't, he just kept it all these years, biding his time until he learned more about Annie.'

Holding his head high, Ralph said, 'I had every right. It's a powerful magical object, that wand. It oughtn't have been in the hands of a little girl. Something like that needs an expert to look after it.' He rearranged his features into something like magnanimity. 'But you're not a little girl anymore, Annie, so I suppose I *could* relent and let you keep the wand, as long as you tell my son to hand over that teapot. And Dora too, of course, just for a little while.' He raised a hand and added, 'Now, I know what you're thinking – but you're wrong. I only need the teapot and Dora for a short while, and it's for a very noble reason. I–'

At first, when Ralph stopped speaking, I thought he was simply trying to think of something more to say, some coaxing words that would convince us it was perfectly safe and reasonable to hand Dora over to him. But as his mouth hung open longer, and longer, and his eyes stared ahead without expression, I realised: Ralph was frozen.

Then, looking at Laine, I saw that *he* was frozen too.

Hugo, though, was fully mobile, and shaking from his head to his toes. 'I ... I didn't mean to do it. I just *thought* it. I thought if only I had the balls to put a freezing spell on them so that you and I could just ... just think. Or maybe, you know, do a runner.' He shrugged pitifully. 'I think it was because I was holding your wand. I think it's very, very strong, Annie. What do we do? Oh crap, oh crap, what do we *do*?'

'Well, first,' I said, gingerly taking my wand from his hand. 'We take this from you before anything else unexpected happens. And second...' I turned my head towards the door. 'We should go down to your office, because it sounds like someone is arriving on the fifth floor.'

∽

NO ONE EVER CAME UP TO THE FIFTH FLOOR — IT WASN'T EVEN listed on the museum map – so to suddenly hear unexpected arrivals was ... odd. Hugo and I ran down the stairs and out through the Griffin-door, to find ourselves face-to-face with two of the fae queen's tallest, strongest-looking guards. I shivered at the sight of them, feeling certain that they could crack us in two with the merest glance.

'Your Majesty.' I stared at her, as the guards parted, and she walked daintily through their middle, entering Hugo's office area to greet us. She wasn't barefoot now, but instead was wearing a pair of leather-soled flip-flops with a pretty design.

'Ah. That's *exactly* what I was looking for.' She smiled at the sight of the teapot, still clutched in Hugo's shaking hands.

Hugo stared at her for a moment, and then said, 'You're the Queen of the Sióga.'

'I am,' she confirmed with a nod.

'You're – you're the most powerful woman in all the realms,' he went on.

'According to most,' she replied.

He gave her a long, awestruck stare, and then held it out to her. 'Take it. Take it, please!' he cried with relief. 'Only don't tell my dad I gave it to you so easily. Say your guards fought me for it.'

'If you think that's necessary, then I shall,' she agreed.

As she handed the teapot to one of her guards, Hugo's whole body sagged. 'Your Majesty,' he said, 'you have to understand that my father – he – well, I'm absolutely sure that he *never* would have gone after this if he knew it was yours.'

She gave him a sympathetic smile. 'Oh, of course. And I hope he tells you often what a very good son you are. I want to say a very big thank you to you both – your friends Jake and Fee were wonderful too, from what I hear. Some members of the White Rabbit Guard have just visited me and filled me in on today's events.'

'Oh, have they now?' I lifted a brow. 'So that's where they went to. Scurried back to their original mistress with their tails between their legs. If they have tails. Do they?'

While the Queen simply laughed, Dora stood up in her cup and said, 'You know, you should really get better guards. They killed Mr Coneen. They betrayed you, and they'll probably do it again. The Cheshire Cat always says your problem is that you're far too nice. Too trustworthy. You need to toughen up, Your Majesty, because not everyone is as nice as you are.'

'Oh, I know.' There was a haunted look in her eyes, as she added, 'Believe me, I know. And I can only apologise for what you've all been through. Ciara's thrall was stronger than I ever knew. My guards insist they were never *really* on her side – they say she got into their heads, made them steal the tea set and murder Mr Coneen.' At the mention of his name, her voice faltered. 'He was a good man. Utterly trustworthy. Unfortunately, he was also so utterly *trusting* that it took him a little too long to see the shenanigans happening under his nose in that prison world. A little like myself, in that regard. But ... we shouldn't wallow on what we cannot change. All I can do now is clean up the mess, and take some measures to ensure it never happens again.'

'You can't have Dora!' Hugo blurted.

The fae queen smiled. 'Of course I can't. Dora is very clearly bonded to Annie. It's rare to see a connection so strong. Ah.' Her smile fell away. 'I see. You defended your father's honour *most* impressively, Hugo, but ... he *did* want the teapot, didn't he? No matter who it rightfully belonged with. And you're afraid that he might also want Dora, in order to use it.' She tilted her head to the side, looking curiously at Hugo. 'And you're also afraid *you* might have done something very stupid in order to stop that from happening.'

I could very nearly feel a breeze as Hugo fluttered his lashes and said, 'You – are you in my head, like Ciara was?'

'No. I would never do that. I'm just ... drawing the obvious conclusions. Annie is your friend, I can see that. And, like most good people, you care deeply about your friends. Deeply enough to go against your father, for once, even though he's quite a scary man.'

The breeze from Hugo's lashes grew stronger, and he didn't seem able to articulate any more words, so I spoke for him, saying, 'Yes, Ralph did want the teapot – no matter what. And to borrow Dora, too, though the goddess knows why. And also...' I held up my wand. 'It seemed like he might have wanted this, too, even though it was never his in the first place. It um ... it's quite a powerful wand, apparently, because Hugo accidentally froze his dad with it, and the museum's treasure hunter too. And now ... now we have no idea what to do about any of it. I mean, I guess we should unfreeze them, but...'

'But then you'll be back to square one.' The Queen sat down into Hugo's chair and spun around a few times before speaking again. 'Well, whilst I feel that the teapot would be safest in my museum – yes, I *will* keep it more heavily guarded this time – I happen to think that the decision is Dora's to make.' She bent forward and patted Dora softly on the head. 'It's your teapot, after all, Dora. If you'd like to live in it, I can find a way to keep you safe from anyone who might want to take advantage of your very special gift.'

Dora shook her head. 'I don't want it. It's more trouble than it's worth. All I really want is my nice comfy cup, but ... Ralph won't be happy about this.'

The Queen looked placidly at the Griffin, who had slid shut as soon as Hugo and I came downstairs. 'Well, if one of you would be so good as to say the password for your sentry over there, I think *I* should pay a little visit to Ralph's office – alone, if you don't mind. I can easily unfreeze him. And I can convince him to do the right thing, while I'm at it.'

'Convince him?' Hugo questioned, finally regaining his voice. 'Look, *I* know that what my dad did today was wrong. He shouldn't have sent Annie on such a dangerous job, he shouldn't have colluded with some dodgy members of your White Rabbit Guard, and he definitely shouldn't have tried to steal this teapot. But Your Majesty, you can't convince my dad of anything.'

The Queen smiled sweetly. 'Trust me, Hugo. When I'm finished with your father, he'll be grateful that I'm not sticking *him* in a prison world. So I'd advise you to grant me admittance to the tower.'

I glanced at the Griffin. Though no one else seemed to notice, he nodded and smiled.

'Okay,' I said. 'I'll do it. I'll let you up.'

CHAPTER 20
Hungry Like the Wolf

When the fae queen and her guards marched up the tower stairs, the Griffin closed behind them, and Hugo and I slumped into the chairs around his desk.

'That was ... weird,' he said.

'Just that bit, or the whole day?'

'Oh, the whole day.' He bent forward, elbows on his desk, shaking his head at me. 'Do you hate me now?'

'Hate you?' I gave him a mystified frown. 'Why would I hate you?'

'Because of what Laine did – what my dad made him do. I'm not stupid, Annie. I might not have Fee's super-hearing, but I can pick up on certain things. Something happened between you and Jake in there. And now...'

'Now he doesn't remember any of it.' My voice sounded about as flat as I felt. 'Hugo, do you ... do you know of any way we could let them in on the secret? Jake and Fee?'

He shook his head, his eyes wide and regretful. For a

while we just sat together in gloomy silence, until a booming voice suddenly said, 'There *is* a way. But I cannot tell you what it is.'

Hugo jumped up from his seat, staring at the statue of the Griffin. Then, patting down his suit, he said, 'Do I still have my skin? Because I think I just jumped out of it. You – you *talked?*'

I looked curiously at the Griffin. 'Yeah, you did.'

The Griffin chuckled deeply. 'So, Annie, would you like to pretend you have never heard me speak before?'

Hugo spun to stare at me. 'You knew he could talk – wait, is it a he?'

'He's a guy, yeah,' I said with a sigh. 'And why he's suddenly decided to let you hear him, I have no idea.'

The statue shrugged his shoulders. 'I feared I would be forever disappointed with Hugo, but I now deem him worthy of my time.' He gave Hugo an impressed smile. 'You finally grew a pair. Standing up to your father, looking out for your friends ... I am almost beginning to like you.'

'I ... thank you?' said Hugo. 'I think.'

'And Dora.' The Griffin looked down upon my familiar, snug in her cup. 'It is very nice to see you reunited with your witch at last.'

Dora gave him a sweet little smile, turned over, and went to sleep.

Chuckling, the Griffin added, 'I am gladdened to see you all returned safely. Though after what Fee and Jake must surely have gone through, it does not seem right that they should forget.'

I stared at him, as something I'd been wondering

about finally clicked into place. 'Griff, you *let* them up, didn't you? Laine wouldn't have forgotten to tell you to close back over behind him.'

Again, he shrugged. 'I calculated the odds of your survival with Laine, versus your chances with your three friends by your side. I made the only decision I could. I have told you, Annie – this museum will never let you down. In return, I would like *you,* now, to keep Fee safe. She is growing gaunt. And hangry. Something is very wrong with her.'

'I know,' I said sadly. 'I think it's this abstinence group she's been going to. It's got her believing she can control the wolf – only in order to do that, she seems to be starving herself. But she's never told me where it is, so...'

'Actually,' said Hugo. 'I think I can figure it out.' He pulled out his phone. 'Fee got a new phone recently. It's got Find My Friends on it, and knowing Fee she won't have disabled that option. We know her meeting's at seven, so I can track her location and you and I can go along, Annie. We'll have plenty of time to make it to Jake's art show afterwards.'

'I...' I hesitated. I didn't like sneaking around, and I definitely didn't want to spy on my friend. But if even the Griffin was worried about her, then maybe it was necessary. 'Okay. We'll do it. Hey, Griff, I met a friend of yours in Wonky Wonderland. He wasn't made of stone, though.'

'Ah. You must mean Gryph. Did he have a message for me?'

'He said to tell you he said: "What's Up?"'

'Oh dear.' The statue's voice grew grave. 'Those are worrying words indeed.'

'Are they?'

'The last time Gryph and I spoke, he told me he would like me to burn in the pits of Hades. Such a friendly greeting makes me wonder if *he* has had a glimpse of the future.'

'Are you saying that you have?' I asked, my curiosity going wild. 'Had a vision of the future?'

He sighed and rolled his eyes. 'Always with the questions, Annie.'

'Always with the frustrating non-answers, Griff,' I countered with a sigh and an eyeroll of my own. 'But … you said there was a way to let Fee and Jake in on the secret.' Before he could interrupt, I added, 'I know, I know – *you* can't tell me what it is. But someone else can, can't they?'

His expression grew positively delighted. 'Finally, you are learning to ask the right questions. When next you see Laine, ask him to introduce you to the man in room two.' Before I could ask anything else, he made a shooing motion and said, 'Now be off, the pair of you. I have stuff to do.'

∽

That evening, when Hugo told me where we were going, I almost changed my mind again. His phone had informed him that Fee's abstinence meeting was taking place in the Samhain Street enclave. Just the mention of that place made me shudder, shiver *and* judder. Samhain

Street was rough — so rough that my grandfather had set up a shop there, selling magical objects, hoping to hide in plain sight. Seeing as he'd been murdered in that very shop, his plan hadn't worked out so well.

I was glad that Dora was fast asleep and snoring. Yeah, I already hated being parted from her, but taking her into a den of deluded werewolves when she'd only just escaped a world of vicious vampires ... well, it seemed like I might be tempting fate. Leaving her at home was the wiser option.

My mother promised to check on her, which put me even more at ease. I'd been worried about how to explain Dora — it was hardly normal for a witch to suddenly gain a familiar at twenty-seven — but as usual, the dormouse's cuteness won the day. My mother was instantly in love, and didn't seem to notice the many gaping holes in my story.

Satisfied that Dora was well looked after, I headed to meet Hugo.

Like Warren Lane, Samhain Street was incredibly misnamed. There was far more than one street in that enclave, and none of them were pretty. The whole place was shrouded in a stinking vapour, coming up off the canal.

We followed Hugo's phone to a part of the enclave called Desperation Row. Somehow, despite being quite some distance from the canal, the air smelled rotten. The abstinence meeting was taking place in a room above one of the area's many casinos, and it was already packed by the time Hugo and I went in and stood at the back.

No one looked at us, because no one could see us.

Hugo had created invisibility spells to shroud us, and he'd also thought to spritz us both with some werewolf pheromones, to disguise our scent.

There were about twenty people crammed into the small room, Fee among them. She was seated right up front, looking impatient for things to begin. Just when I thought she was about to burst with frustration, a raggedy curtain was pulled aside by a skinny woman. There, on a makeshift stage, a large, hairy man was revealed. The dark hairs of his arms and chest were visible through his barely-buttoned shirt and rolled up sleeves. A poster on the wall showed an image of him in transition, halfway between man and wolf.

Although I'd never seen anyone quite like this man before, there was something about him – something that I strongly disliked. Just the sight of him put me on edge, and when he began to speak I hated him even more.

'For those of you who do not know me yet, I am Herr Wind,' he said to the crowd. 'I see you are all looking at this terrible picture. I know you will barely believe it, but zis truly is me, during my dark days when I could not control myself. Here, I am pictured in ze most secret parts of ze Black Forest, where werewolves and vampires roam. Oh, but even then I knew I must find a way to break myself from zis curse. And so, I journeyed from my Black Forest homeland and wandered far and wide, in search of a cure. Some of you already know zat I vas successful. After many years and great expense and danger, I have at last perfected the most vunderful No-Turn potion in ze supernatural world.'

As the skinny woman opened up a box filled with

bottles, Herr Wind beamed around the room. 'And for any newcomers who have not yet tried it, you can avail of the discounted rate of five gold rounds per bottle.'

I couldn't see Hugo right now, but if I could, I imagine we would have been sharing a stunned-mullet glance. Five gold rounds was a *lot* of money for a No-Turn potion. If that was the discounted price, then how much more expensive was it for the regular users? No wonder Fee was still working at the Hungry Hippy, even with her recent pay bump. Herr Wind was fleecing everyone in this room.

'I vish so much zat ze ingredients for zis cure came cheaper,' he said, as one or two people at the back looked uncertain. 'I promise you all, I am only covering my costs here. Zis potion is so vunderful, in fact, zat eventually you will not need to take it anymore – think of how much money you will save then!'

He nodded kindly, as the more hesitant members joined the queue and began to purchase their potions.

'Now, remember, zis potion is only part of ze cure,' he said, once every bottle was gone. 'For it to be at its most effective, ve must also be careful to refrain from ze four poisons. Can anyone tell me – vat are ze four poisons?'

One group member eagerly stuck up his hand. 'Me, me, I know it! The first poison is any food which rouses the passions. The second is alcohol, the third is laughter, and–' His face grew pale and he began to sway. Holding onto his head, he said, 'I don't know what's wrong with me. I've forgotten the fourth one. Just ... if I could sit a minute so I feel less faint, I'm sure I'll be able to remember it.'

While some others helped him into a seat, I turned to where I thought Hugo was standing and whispered, '*Laughter* is a poison?'

'No wonder she's not herself,' he whispered back. 'This group would drive anyone round the bend. Oh, look – she's standing up.'

He was right. Fee had stood up and raised her hand. As Herr Wind turned to her, she called out, 'And dancing, Herr Wind! Dancing is the fourth poison, because it can create an unhealthy level of fervour which could lead to wolfing out.'

'Yes, yes, my clever little Fee-Fee,' said Herr Wind, rubbing his palms together. 'Oh, you are truly my greatest success, Fee-Fee. You are looking healthier than ever. Vud you, my bestest and most reformed werewolf, like to lead us in a round of the Abstinence Song?'

Fee kicked off the sing-along, with many others standing up and joining in (some were a little too weak, and remained in their seats). It was only when Herr Wind began to sing that I knew, finally, why I had developed such an instant and visceral dislike of this man.

'Hugo!' I hissed. 'Are you still beside me?'

'Of course. Are you still beside me?'

I decided not to resort to sarcasm. I just said 'Yeah,' and then, 'Hugo, I don't think there's really any such person as Herr Wind. I think he's using a glamour spell to disguise himself. And I think – oh crud, I can't believe I'm about to say this – but I think that's my dad up there.'

Hugo was silent a moment, then he said, 'Annie, are you sure?'

'Well, no, because it would be bloody mental if it was him, wouldn't it? But ... I recognise his actions. The way he moves. The way he *sings*. My dad loved making up stupid songs just like this one when I was a kid. There was one about how bananas are demon food, another about honey being a gateway sugar. And he always had that same fervent look in his eyes, because *he* gets happier when he's sucking the joy of life from everyone around him. It's just how he's wired. It's him, Hugo, I know it is.'

'Herr Wind *does* have a touch of the crazed cult leader about him,' Hugo agreed. 'But there's one way to be sure. Can I borrow your wand for a revelation spell? I somehow get the feeling it'll be a much stronger spell than anything I could do on my own.'

I nodded and passed him my wand. Still with his own invisibility intact, Hugo pointed it at the stage and whispered, 'Foilsigh.'

The man instantly changed, his glamour falling away as he became taller, slightly less hairy, and far, far paler and thinner.

With a gasp, Fee dropped the potion she'd just paid far too much money for, and said, 'You're not Herr Wind! You're Windflower Egan! You're Annie's dad!' After blinking in shock for a few moments, she looked around the room and said, 'He's a fraud! This man is a stinking, thieving conman! I'm calling the Wayfarers right now!'

Windflower knew, then, that the jig was up. Under normal circumstances, he might have done a runner. But Hugo still had my very powerful wand in his hand, so he pointed it again, freezing my father on the spot.

A LITTLE WHILE LATER, WE STOOD OUT ON THE STREET TALKING with Fee. Hugo had revealed himself to her first, right after she was done with the Wayfarers. I'd been a little terrified to reveal myself – it was my dad, after all, who was cheating her. But once she'd eaten the burgers Hugo had bought her while we waited, her mood had improved a lot.

'I can't believe you guys went to so much trouble, just for me,' she said, wiping her mouth and looking more satisfied than I'd ever seen her. 'Especially when I've been such a gullible fool. I can't *believe* I never copped on that Herr Wind was actually Windflower. I mean, now it seems so obvious, but I was completely taken in.'

'You're not mad with me?' I asked in a shaky voice.

She crushed me into one of her super-tight embraces (maybe the hug was my punishment). 'You great big silly mare!' she said. 'Of course I'm not mad with you. I know what it's like to have a crappy dad.'

'You do?' I mumbled curiously against her shoulder. 'Sounds like we all have crappy dads, doesn't it? No offence, Hugo.' I tossed him a guilty glance before turning back to Fee and saying, 'Wanna talk about it?'

'Nope,' she said firmly, letting go of me. 'Not right now.' While I caught my breath, she added, 'Anyway, we should go check on our other friend, shouldn't we? Jake's art show will be starting soon.'

'We should definitely go,' said Hugo. 'He said there'll be wine and cheese – I could really do with a glass of red after the day I've had.'

'Me too,' Fee agreed, as she linked arms with us. 'I think I'll let my hair down a bit tonight, actually. Might as well have fun before I start the search for another abstinence group.'

Hugo laughed. Fee didn't.

'You're joking?' Hugo questioned, his laughter falling away as he looked at her with concern. 'That ... that was a joke, right?'

'Mm-hm, mm-hm, totally joking,' she said, her voice pitched a little too high. 'Come on guys – let's get to Jake's.'

CHAPTER 21
THE FOUR OF US

A little while later, I hovered at the doorway of Fuelling Art, holding tight to Dora's cup as she peered out over the rim. I'd told Hugo and Fee to go on ahead while I checked on the dormouse, and now here I was, *with* her. She'd been wide awake when I went back to the flat, and it had taken me a few minutes longer than I thought it would to catch up with the others (because Dora thought I should put on some lipstick, style my hair and – most importantly – wash off the werewolf pheromones).

Now that I was up to my familiar's standards, and less likely to attract a pack of amorous werewolves my way, I intended to head straight over to Hugo and Fee. When I saw how close they were sitting, though, talking quietly together, I decided not to interrupt; instead, I inched my way in past them and did a slow circuit of the room.

Fuelling Art was buzzing, filled up with arty-looking types sipping tiny coffees and huge glasses of wine, trotting about from painting to painting, sculpture to sculpture, loudly talking in words I didn't understand. I'd learned a *little* about art in my Magical History course, because any respectable conservator of magical artefacts needs to know how to spot an evil portrait. But after a few stilted conversations, it was obvious that I was *so* out of my depth.

When Jake broke away from a group and came over to me, though, I felt instantly at ease.

'Who's this?' he asked with a bright smile as he gently rubbed Dora's head. She responded happily, pressing further into him and grinning.

'This is Dora, my familiar,' I explained, feeling my spirits plummet. After everything we'd been through today, he now had no idea who she was. Sure, I'd known that this was how things would be, but it didn't make it any easier.

'Well, you're just as pretty as your witch, aren't you Dora?' said Jake, his face turning bright red as soon as he'd spoken the words. Clearing his throat, he straightened up and said, 'We kind of rushed out of the museum this afternoon. I didn't get a chance to say how glad I was.'

'Glad?'

'That you didn't get bitten. I wouldn't wish that on anyone. I've felt so weird all afternoon. I fell asleep for a couple of hours, and the dreams...' He shuddered. 'Anyway, I'm sure it'll wear off soon enough. There's something, actually, that I should tell you. I mean, maybe it doesn't matter, but given what we were talking about this morning, I...' He trailed off, clearly struggling to find the words to say whatever it was he wanted to.

About ten seconds into his very long pause, a pretty, black-haired woman came over and snaked her arm around his waist. I'd only met her once before, but I would recognise her anywhere. This was Karen, Jake's ex. Now, though, given how physically comfortable she was with him, I was wondering if their relationship status had changed.

'Hey there,' she said, grinning at him. 'Some woman from the Berry coven wants to buy Brighter Mornings. I told her I'd ask you how much it is.'

'That one's not for sale,' he told her with a grunt, shaking her off. Lowering his voice, he added, 'Alex displayed it without asking me. Anyway, I thought you were leaving.'

She flinched, looking hurt. She didn't answer him, but turned to me instead, giving me a friendly smile and saying, 'It's Annie, isn't it? Jake's friend from the museum. It's so nice of you all to come tonight and support him. I was just talking to Fee a few minutes ago. She's lovely, isn't she?'

'Yeah,' I agreed. 'She's lovely. I em ... I think I'm going to go and grab a drink. Do you two want anything?'

They both shook their heads, Jake looking relieved as I walked away. I was a little relieved, too, just to get away from them. If I'd known she was going to be here tonight, I would have been tempted to give it a miss. I had no idea if she'd turned up uninvited, or if Jake had changed his mind and asked her to come. Either way, it was none of my business. One day, if what the Griffin said was true,

I'd be able to tell him absolutely everything, but until then ... maybe it was best if I just left him be.

'She's not as pretty as you,' Dora said, giving me a sweet smile.

'Oh, you're such a liar.' I bent to kiss her head. 'And I love you for it.'

We spent the next half hour wandering around and looking at the art. Fee and Hugo were still having an intense conversation, and Jake and Karen seemed to be arguing, but with Dora for company I could never feel alone. She kept up a running commentary on the rest of the crowd, making me laugh out loud at times.

When I came to the painting called Brighter Mornings, I stopped laughing, and simply stared. I didn't know what you would call the style. There were blurry but beautiful strokes, making up a rainy-day street scene of Poppy Lane, as viewed from the window of Jake's flat. I'd seen this painting a little while back, but it had become something entirely different between then and now. Because now, there was one brighter, less blurry subject, right at the centre of the piece. It was a woman sitting out on a bench in front of the Hungry Hippy. The clouds had parted above her, and the sun shone down on where she sat. She wore a yellow raincoat and a wide-brimmed hat, and she was hunched over a coffee and reading a book.

'That's your raincoat, Annie,' said Dora in hushed tones. 'And your hat – I saw them in your wardrobe. It's you. Jake's painted you.'

She was right, and I knew it. The thought of Jake looking out at me, painting me, while I took a break after the morning rush at the restaurant ... it brought a lump to my throat. He'd painted this before we kissed, and I couldn't help wondering what he would paint now. Would our experiences in Ciara's world filter into his dreams, becoming part of his consciousness, or would it all simply vanish?

'I thought you were sleeping while I was out,' I said to Dora, wiping away a tear.

'I was. And then I woke up and had a nose about. You don't mind, do you? Your house is my house, right?'

'Right.' I nuzzled her head, still staring at the painting. I probably would have kept on staring for a long while more, but a shadow fell over me. Turning a little, I saw Laine standing behind me.

'He's made you look beautiful,' he said, his voice gruff.

Bristling, I asked him: 'What are you doing here?'

'I needed to talk to you. To explain. I figured if I came here, I might catch you unawares – you're hardly going to scream at me and tell me to get lost on Jake's big night, are you? You won't want to ruin it for him.'

'I'm not sure whether to be impressed or horrified by your reasoning.'

'Desperate times and all that,' he said, a pained expression on his face. 'I know you probably won't believe me when I say this, but I really am sorry, Annie. I should have told you I had a way of communicating with Ralph. And I did know more than I let you in on, about the job. I mean, I didn't *know*, not exactly, but I definitely suspected there was more to it than what Ralph was telling me. I knew something was up when he wanted me to train you so hard – and I *definitely* suspected him of shenanigans when he told me I should grill you about Dora whenever you were standing near the mirror.' He smiled down at her. 'But you found her in the end, and you got to keep her. Maybe that's all that matters?'

Dora let out a growl. I didn't know that dormice *could* growl, but mine certainly could.

Sighing, Laine said, 'Yeah, I guess I deserved that.'

'Yeah,' I agreed. 'You did. What happened with the faery queen?'

'Oh, you know ...' He chuckled darkly. 'Ralph insisted he was going to give her the teapot all along. He concocted some ridiculous story about how he was only pretending to work with the White Rabbit Guard, and that it was all part of his master plan to get the teapot back into her hands. Then, when she left, he gave me a particularly grim scowl before taking off to who knows where. He told me to keep training you, though, so at least we have many more arguments to look forward to. I assume you *are* staying at the museum?'

If he'd asked me that question a few hours ago, I would probably have laughed in his face and stormed off, swearing never to come back to the museum again – because I really *was* exhausted with it all. But now, after what the Griffin said...

I searched my brain for ways to broach the question I needed to ask. Before I could come up with anything, Laine said, 'I think I know why Ralph wanted that teapot, by the way.'

'You do?'

He nodded bleakly. 'I do. I think he wanted it for the

Donor's Ball. It's coming up soon. The richest people attend, and at the end of the night, they – hopefully – donate enough money to keep the museum running.'

'Ah.' I was beginning to understand. 'And with the magic of the teapot, Ralph could have convinced them of anything – like, maybe he could have given them a very strong urge to be extra generous.'

Laine nodded. 'Exactly. And without it, he's got to rely on someone else to schmooze the donors. His manager.'

'His *manager*? Laine, I thought Ralph was in charge of the museum.'

'Most of the time he is. But you must have figured out by now, Annie, that there's a lot more going on in that place than meets the eye. You'll be meeting him soon enough – if Ralph gives you access to room number two.'

'Room two?' I gazed at him, blinking, my heart running wild. That was the room the Griffin had mentioned. 'In the central tower? Who is this guy, Laine? Are you saying he lives *in* the tower?'

He didn't answer me, but stared across the room to where Jake and Karen were still arguing. 'They did well in there today, didn't they? Fee, Hugo ... Jake?'

'They did,' I told him. 'All of them, but Jake especially. Without him, I might've been dinner for Tweedledo and Tweedledon't.'

'Huh.' He shook his head. 'I would have sworn he'd fade away and leave the rest of you to fend for yourselves. I guess you never can tell.'

Somewhere in one of his pockets, a bell rang urgently.

'That'll be Ralph,' he said with a sigh. 'Which means I don't have time to tell you anything else right now. But I'll see you soon, okay? And even if Ralph doesn't allow me to do it, I *will* make sure you meet his manager. Because Annie, that guy, he might be able to grant you your biggest wish.' He glanced at Jake again. Raising his hand, preparing to click his fingers and teleport away, he added, 'I just hope it's worth it.'

~

When Laine vanished, I sank down into the chair nearest the Brighter Mornings painting. While I was looking at it, a great big soft head landed on my lap. I grinned at Wim's arrival. 'Hey there,' I said, softly stroking the head of Jake's familiar. 'You having fun, buddy?'

The Old English Sheepdog let out a loud, mournful sigh. 'I wish you were my witch's girlfriend, Annie.'

'Oh.' I felt a sad little flutter in my chest and stomach. 'That's ... I don't know what to say to that.'

'Jake's much happier when he's with you. He wasn't even a little bit invisible earlier on, when you were talking to him. But look at him now.'

I followed the dog's gaze. Some music had started up, and Karen was leading Jake onto a section of floor that had been cleared for dancing. At least I *thought* she was leading Jake. He seemed to be fading rather a lot, so all I could really make out was the lower part of his legs.

'I second that,' said Alex, taking a seat next to me. 'Jake would be much better off with someone like you. Karen's trouble.'

I frowned, focusing more carefully on Karen. She looked far too perfect to be trouble. 'She seems really nice, but I've only met her twice, so...'

'Trust me,' said Alex. 'I've got experience.'

'Like what?' I asked, unable to disguise my interest.

He shook his head. 'Never mind. My mouth runs away with me when I'm on the bourbon. Hey, your familiar looks nice.' Alex scratched Dora's head, and she responded with a smile. 'She doesn't look all judgy, like mine.' He pointed to a basket next to the cash register, where a tiny Pomeranian was lying in a ball. She had her eyes on Alex, and she definitely looked like she was judging him.

He was really quite drunk, and a wicked part of me wanted to take advantage of that and ask him more about Karen. But just as I opened my mouth, Hugo rushed over.

Hugging me from behind (perhaps he was a little drunk too), he said, 'I want to ask Fee to dance, but ... I don't think it'll look very professional if I ask her to dance with me on my own. Come join us?'

'Don't be an idiot, Hugo,' I told him with a gentle laugh. 'Just ask her. I guarantee you she'll say yes.'

He blushed deeply. 'Well ... I don't know about that. Anyway, it'd be kind of icky of me to take advantage when I'm sprayed all over with werewolf pheromones. It's probably the whole reason she's so interested in everything I have to say tonight.'

I gave his shoulder a squeeze. 'I don't think that's true, but okay – I'll get up and dance. And Wim's coming too.'

'And Alex.' Alex held up a hand. 'Because Alex seriously needs to burn off all the bourbon he's had.'

'And me.' Dora yawned and stretched. 'But you might have to put me in your handbag and swing me around, because I don't want my cup to get crushed.'

So we headed out on to the dancefloor, and threw ourselves around like crazy. Jake dragged Karen over to join us, but after a while she and Alex drifted off to get more drinks. A few minutes later, Wim and Dora disappeared into a corner to discuss tennis and croquet.

After that, it was just the four of us, dancing. I felt a buzz of happiness, now that we were together again, just like we'd been in that wonky world of Queen Ciara's. All of my worries seemed to fade away: the man in room number two, the mystery of the ghost in my locket … none of it seemed nearly as daunting anymore.

Maybe it was because I'd had some wine, or because the music was improving my mood, but that night while we danced, I felt sure that as long as we had each other, everything else would fall into place.

∼

THANK YOU FOR READING. IF YOU ENJOYED THIS BOOK, YOU'LL be happy to know that the next adventure for Annie and friends, *Vampire's Ball,* is coming soon.

If you'd like to be among the first to hear when it's released, you can sign up for my newsletter at my website: https://aaalbright.com

Printed in Great Britain
by Amazon